THE DYRYSGOL HORROR

Borgo Press Books by EDMUND GLASBY

The Dyrysgol Horror and Other Weird Tales

THE DYRYSGOL HORROR

AND OTHER WEIRD TALES

EDMUND GLASBY

THE BORGO PRESS

MMXII

THE DYRYSGOL HORROR

FIRST EDITION

Published by Wildside Press LLC

www.wildsidebooks.com

DEDICATION

To Katherine and Robert

CONTENTS

THE DYRYSGOL HORROR

An ancestral terror from the past had returned to prey on the villagers.

Thunder rumbled briefly along the distant horizon, followed shortly after by a sudden flash of brilliance. The moon drifted behind a voluminous mass of dark cloud. Lightning flashed again, high in the heavens, as Detective Inspector Bernard Owen tried to concentrate on steering the car through the increasingly atrocious conditions. Several narrow farm tracks led off the road, but none of these were signposted, and most were little more than rutted paths leading apparently nowhere across deserted moorland and low, rounded hills that brooded oppressively on the skyline. Despite the fact that he had the car headlights on full beam, in the heavy rain, it was proving nigh on impossible to see anything clearly, giving the passing trees on either side a shadowy and menacing appearance.

He had been out this way only once before, and it was with a growing sense of trepidation that he noticed how the surrounding countryside seemed to grow more sinister and sombre in its overall aspect. The car lurched and bounced over several potholes, and the road had now become so narrow that the thorny hedges slashed and tore at the vehicle on both sides.

Another flash of lightning threw the dark trees into sudden stark relief, making them appear for a moment like startled ghosts. This was followed by a crash of thunder that seemed to shake the ground. Moonlight filtered through the dense, ominous clouds, throwing grotesque shadows across the landscape and illuminating the tall and foreboding shape of Dyrysgol Castle that now reared high on a hill directly ahead in an eldritch glow.

Owen brought the car to a stop.

There was a tight burning sensation at the back of his temples. The mere sight of the partially ruined castle set atop the hill before him, with its cracked and splintered towers and its crenellations silhouetted against the full moon, filled his stomach with a sudden wave of fear which threatened to push all other thoughts out of his mind, almost overwhelming him completely. His heart began to hammer against his ribs like a frightened beast. He closed his eyes tightly and tried to think calmly and logically.

Despite the fact that he was a Detective Inspector, there was no denying the fact that he was scared and, not for the first time that evening, he wished that he had brought some of his constables along with him, or at the very least, some of the local villagers. For, once more, there had been a disappearance—this time a farmer from one of the outlying farmsteads—and it was his duty to carry out an investigation.

As he sat in his car, staring up at the dark castle, he deliberated on the way in which he would initiate his questioning with Viscount Ravenwood, a man whom he had only met once before and a man who, clearly, was regarded with a great deal of suspicion and dislike amongst the highly superstitious villagers. There was no denying the fact that Ravenwood had done little to dispel the notorious reputation both he and his ancestors had earned over the centuries. For he had remained aloof and indifferent to local affairs, preferring instead to shun all contact with the village and to dispatch his manservant, Franklins, whenever the need arose to procure goods and necessities.

Owen reflected on this, pondering just how strange it was for a man of reputed wealth to live the life of a self-imposed hermit. Had his inherited wealth somehow disposed him against living with people whom he believed were below his standing? Or was there something else? After all, he could have sold or even abandoned the castle and moved to sunnier climes. It was what he would have done if their positions were reversed.

The rain outside was becoming heavier, although the thunder and lightning seemed to have eased somewhat. Gently chewing his bottom lip, Owen stirred the car into life once more and continued the long, uphill drive towards the castle.

Passing through the entrance gateway, undoubtedly a once-grandiose structure but now reduced to but two columns surmounted by small, bloated, winged gargoyles, he could see, through the darkness, that there did appear to be lights on in the ground floor of the castle. The grounds he was now driving through levelled out slightly and he could see what appeared to be several ruinous, vine-festooned burial edifices, emerging, spectrally, from the darkness. Cracked statues lined the approaching drive, leering at him from the shadows, their faces seemingly frozen in anger at this trespass. Some were twisted and fractured, little more than shattered heaps of half-buried statuary, whilst others were huge and towering, giant shapes laden with malice, monstrous idols that stood sentinel over the approach to Dyrysgol Castle.

What a place! Owen doubted if there was anywhere else in Wales that even resembled it, and as he drew his car up alongside the black, hearse-like vehicle that Franklins occasionally drove into the village, a sudden compulsion to turn the car around and head back flooded into his mind. It was small wonder, he thought, how this place, and its enigmatic owner, had managed to earn such a bad reputation. It was muttered in the village, and indeed, to some extent, in the wider district, that the Ravenwood family had long been associated with devil worship. It was held to be a distinct possibility that the current viscount still entertained such foul practices.

Swallowing a lump in his throat, he reluctantly got out of the car and made a dash for the main entrance. He was just about to rap on the large, ornately carved knocker set in the middle of the iron-banded and studded door, when, to his surprise, he heard the sound of bolts being withdrawn from inside, and the door swung open, its un-oiled hinges squeaking protestingly, the sound not unlike that from a nest of dying rats.

Franklins, the manservant, looked at Owen disapprovingly. It was impossible to read what thoughts were going through him, for his face was blank and impassive. He was tall and slim, well dressed, but there seemed to be nothing in his eyes, neither malice nor welcome.

After an uneasy and slightly embarrassing moment, Owen said: "Good evening. I'd like to have a word with Lord Ravenwood, if he's available." Despite the fact that he was here pursuing a line of enquiry, and that he possessed all of the legal backing necessary to conduct his investigation, he felt uncomfortable just being here. Get a grip of yourself, he thought sternly. He was a Detective Inspector, had been for over twenty years, and besides, there was nothing to be afraid of here, or so he thought.

Franklins stared at him for a moment longer, whatever recollection he had of Owen's past visit, several months ago, not registering in the slightest, and it was abundantly clear that he was unrehearsed with any form of etiquette when it came to making a guest feel welcome. Eventually, he said in a monotone voice: "His Lordship is in. But he's not to be disturbed."

"I'm here on official police business," said Owen. "There's been a disappearance. Another one. Now, if you'd be so good as to inform Lord Ravenwood that I'm here, I'd like to have a word." An undertone of authority had returned to his voice. It would do no good, at a time like this, for the other to think that he was incapable of carrying out his duties.

"Very well. Wait a moment, please." Franklins turned swiftly, and made his way along the wood panelled hallway, the walls of which were richly decorated with tapestries, antlers, and heraldic shields. He then disappeared into a doorway on the left.

Owen stepped inside and waited for the other to return.

A minute or two passed before the tall, dark-haired form of Viscount Ravenwood stepped out from beyond the door with his manservant in tow. He was an aristocratic-looking man of handsome and yet sharp features possibly somewhere in his early forties. He wore a dark grey, strangely-padded jacket and a pair of black trousers. A thin film of sweat covered his face and strands of black hair hung damply against his forehead. It was clear that he had been engaged in some form of physical activity. But Owen's eyes were not concentrated so much on the man's appearance as on the heavy and dangerous-looking broadsword he carried in his right hand.

"Lord Ravenwood." Owen stepped forward and offered his hand. "It's a pleasure to meet with you once more. I hope this is not an inconvenience."

Ravenwood paused for a moment, throwing a brief, untrusting glance at the Detective Inspector's hand, before transferring his broadsword to his left hand and shaking it. "Inspector, I understand that there's been another disappearance from the village. Is that correct?" His manner and accent were polite, precise, and yet somehow rather chilling.

Owen nodded his head slightly. "I'm afraid so."

"Hmm. And am I also to understand, as this is your second visit, that I'm under some suspicion?"

Owen felt uncomfortable under the other's dark scrutiny. There was something unreadable in the man's piercing gaze—something dark and slightly sinister that engendered the uneasy feeling within him that this man had seen horrors not fit for human sight. "This is all purely routine. I'm sure you understand the gravity of the situation. I was wondering if we could just have a little talk."

Ravenwood contained a laugh. "A little talk, is it? What you actually mean is can I explain where I've been all evening, and whether or not I had anything to do with the unfortunate's death."

"Who said anything about anyone being killed?" Owen countered, making a mental note of what the other had just said. It was little things like this that often revealed the true details about another's involvement. It never ceased to amaze him how even the most astute could talk themselves into difficulty. It was just a question of giving them enough rope—

"Come now, Inspector. Surely you don't believe that all of the people who've disappeared over the past year or so are still alive, do you? Where do you think they've gone? Why would they 'up-sticks' as it were, leaving their families and loved ones behind? Of course they're dead. You know this as well as I. But please, why don't you go into the study and make yourself comfortable whilst I change into something less intimidating. Franklins will show you the way." He turned and made his way back along the corridor.

"If you'd follow me," said the manservant, ushering Owen towards one of the doors that led off from the main entrance hall. He led the way along a wide corridor, hung at intervals with weird trophies which successive generations of Ravenwoods had obviously collected from all over the world.

"What's with the sword?" inquired Owen.

Franklins turned. "Sorry?"

"The sword. Does the viscount make a habit of walking around his house armed such as that?"

"No, sir. It's just that he always insists on an hour's swordplay most evenings. He follows quite a vigorous routine of both physical and mental exercise, as did his father. Here we are."

From the doorway, Owen could see that inside the study there was a warm fire blazing in the open hearth. The walls were lined with stags' heads and bookcases, the contents of which appeared old, yet well looked after. In one corner, at the far end, stood a suit of anti-quated plate mail armour. Opposite it was an upright, stuffed bear. A long oaken table, surrounded by several chairs, lay in the centre of the room, and a large, dusty chandelier hung from above, lending the place an air of forgotten and now long-lost opulence. A pair of crossed halberds hung above the fireplace.

"If you'd just wait here," said Franklins gesturing to one of the chairs. "I'm sure his Lordship will not be long. Would you care for a drink?"

"Not whilst I'm on duty. Thanks all the same." Owen strode over to one of the chairs and sat down, casting his eyes over the numerous collections and antiques that adorned the walls. This was the same room he had been in the last time he had paid the viscount a visit, and from the looks of it nothing had changed in the slightest. Just how many rooms were there in the castle, he thought. Twenty? A hundred? Although some of the castle, certainly when seen from the outside, appeared to have suffered greatly from the ravages of time, it was abundantly evident that many of the interior living spaces were perfectly functional.

On the table in front of him, within arm's reach, there were numerous books. There was also a very antiquated globe, a collection of strange brass paperweights and a silver tray bearing a large crystal-cut decanter and several empty wine glasses. Nonchalantly, he picked one of them up and spun it in his fingers so that the harsh glare from the overhead lights was reflected in a million splintered rainbow shards off its faceted surface. A thousand eyes of fire, green and blue and red, winked at him mockingly. Hastily, he set it down on the table again.

After a few minutes, he heard a door close and the sound of approaching footsteps.

Now dressed in a velvet smoking jacket and slippers, Ravenwood stepped into the study. He looked far more relaxed, and some of the sternness seemed to have dissipated from his face. "Sorry to have kept you waiting, Inspector," he said, trying to sound as genial as possible for that late hour of the evening. "I take it that Franklins has offered you a drink?" he said, removing the top from the decanter.

"Not for me, thanks."

"As you wish." Ravenwood poured himself a glass of wine and then slid into one of the chairs facing the other. "Now, Inspector, how can I be of assistance?"

"Well, that's just it," began Owen uncertainly. "To tell you the truth, I'm not really sure. The facts as they stand have me truly baffled, and all that I can tell you with any certainty is that over the past few months there have been nine disappearances from the nearby village and its outlying farmsteads. Now, as I said at our last visit, I'm not from Dyrysgol. My headquarters are in Tregaron, some twenty miles away, and I'd be the first to admit that things are more than a little strange around here."

"You're referring to the locals?"

Owen gave a half-hearted smile. "Well, in a way, I suppose. You undoubtedly know what they're like better than me. Simple people with simple outlooks. Anyhow, they seem to have formed the opinion that, well—"

He hesitated, unsure how to complete what it was that he wanted to say.

"That I'm in league with the Devil?" Ravenwood interrupted, trying to keep his voice even. "And that, no doubt, it is I who am responsible for the disappearances. No doubt they have told you that I am a sorcerer, conjuring demons from the bottommost pits of Hell, or perhaps a necromancer, raising the dead from the nearby graveyard in order to fulfil my diabolical schemes. I daresay there are some who claim to have seen me with a gathering of witches up on Bryn Garwynn, dancing by firelight around the stone circle there." He took a measured sip from his wine glass.

Owen cleared his throat. "Something like that. I suppose if we look at it from their perspective, it's not that difficult to form such a belief. You never venture out and you'd have to admit that this property is unusual."

"And that's the basis on which to judge another's character? Come now, Inspector, surely you can see, as a man of logic, that the superstitions and the fears are all in their minds. I admit that I am somewhat reclusive, preferring my own company to that of others, but as far as I'm aware, that is not a crime. Now, I understand fully that the spate of disappearances has undoubtedly heightened their concerns, and I can see in your eyes that you share their prejudice against me."

"No, that's not true," said Owen, shaking his head. "I look at everything impartially, based on the evidence that it's my duty to gather. And so far, I have nine people unaccounted for, all of whom seem to have disappeared at or around the time of the full moon."

Ravenwood spread out the fingers of his right hand, looking down for a moment in pensive thought at the signet ring he wore before looking across directly at the other. "A most tragic set of circumstances, and I'll obviously help you in any way that I can, but, as you yourself pointed out, I seldom leave the castle and I'm afraid my assistance may be of little use."

Owen was stumped. If there was any truth in what the other was saying, and without evidence to the contrary it seemed as though there was, then surely he was pursuing a dead end here. He could probably go as far as ordering a search of the castle, to see if any of the missing people were being kept here against their wills, but he reasoned that such a course of action would not be fruitful and it would take time to authorise and conduct. Time in which Ravenwood could destroy whatever evidence there may or may not be.

He was just about to speak, when something large brushed against his legs under the table, causing him to jerk back in surprise. Looking down, he was rather startled to see the large head of a night-black dog, staring up at him, its saliva-flecked jaws ridged with jagged white teeth.

Ravenwood noticed the worried look on the other's face. "Don't be alarmed, Inspector. Wolf has been well-trained, as a guard dog that is. He's merely come to say hello." He gave a wintry smile that failed to put the other at ease.

With a slightly trembling hand, Owen reached out and patted the heavily panting, vicious-looking creature. Desperately, he tried to marshal his turbulent thoughts, to reach some kind of decisive plan of action. He had ventured out here in the hope that Ravenwood might be able to offer some insight into the rash of disappearances. But it seemed that the man knew nothing. That being the case, there was little reason for him to remain a moment longer. Additionally, he did not like the look of the dog. He made to get up from his chair. "I'll take my leave of you then, Lord Ravenwood. If anything should come to your attention regarding these disappearances, I'll be staying at the inn in the village for the next few days if you should wish to contact me."

"Very good. Before you go, Inspector, may I just say that I'd appreciate it if you were to offer my condolences to the relatives at this troubling time. And once again, may I reaffirm that I am not the monster that the villagers take me for. The real monster—is still out there." He pointed towards the lead-latticed study window where the rain and the wind lashed and howled, and grotesque shadows cast from the trees and bushes outside wildly cavorted.

* * * * * *

"I don't suppose Ravenwood said much, did he?" asked the innkeeper, pouring Owen a glass of whisky. "I told you he were a queer one. Living up there in that godforsaken castle, all alone except for that oddball, Franklins." He pushed the glass towards the Inspector. "Here."

"Thanks. Good health." Owen took a measured sip. The fiery liquid went down into his stomach and expanded into a cloud of warmth. He took another sip and rested the glass on the counter. "He didn't have much to say, if that's what you're asking." About him, some dozen or so other patrons were sat about drinking and talking quietly amongst themselves, their voices little more than hushed mutters. Under normal circumstances, there should have been a hubbub of activity; laughing and joking, perhaps a few card games or a friendly dispute over a game of darts, but here hung an air of depression and fear, with anger bubbling just below the surface. He sensed that they were waiting to hear a full-blown account of his visit. To perhaps provide them with cause to mobilise and march on the castle in order to vent their superstition-fuelled wrath; to bring mob justice with flaming torches and pitchforks like in the Mediaeval days. They needed a scapegoat, and he knew that things could get out of hand quite easily. His thoughts were validated when a gruff voice from behind him called out:

"It's him, I tell ye! He's the one responsible. To hell with the Ravenwoods!"

Owen turned, just in time to see a stocky, well-built man with a huge bushy black beard slam his tankard down on the table at which he sat. Ale and foam flew.

"Steady, Pat. Steady!" exclaimed the innkeeper. "We all know that your boy was one of them that's disappeared, but—"

"He were only fourteen!" the thickset man shouted.

"How many more will there be before someone is brought to account?" He threw an accusatory glance at Owen. "Can you tell us that, Inspector? Just how many more innocents will Ravenwood claim before someone does something?"

"There's no proof whatsoever to implicate him in any of these wrongdoings," said Owen, raising his voice in order that the gathered men could hear him well. "He claims to have no knowledge regarding these disappearances. And until any evidence comes up to the contrary, there is absolutely no reason to suspect him. Now, if you all just calm down a minute, I will explain how I plan to proceed from here. In the morning, I expect two constables to be arriving from Tregaron to assist in my investigations. We'll be meticulously going over all the details, trying to piece together what evidence there is in order to—"

With a crash, the door to the inn was flung wide, and a rain-soaked man stumbled forward, prompting all eyes to turn towards him.

Owen and the innkeeper rushed forward, catching the man as he slumped down. There was a look of sheer horror on his face; his eyes were wide and bulging, and he was trembling violently.

"It's old Edwin from the other side of the valley. He looks like death," said the innkeeper, guiding the unfortunate into a chair by the fire. He turned to one of the men nearby. "Get him a large brandy. Hurry, man!"

A large brandy was soon thrust into the shaking hands of the old man. For a moment, he looked at it blankly, as though unsure why it was there before taking a large gulp. He shivered, convulsively, whether due to the cold and the soaking he had obviously received or whether due to something else, Owen was unsure, although he highly suspected the latter. After a minute or two some semblance of lucidity began to creep back into him. He jerked upright, eyes staring wildly around him.

Edwin took another hefty drink of brandy. He tried desperately to gather his distraught emotions. It was abundantly clear that he had experienced something—something that had given him the fright of his life. "It was as I was coming back along the road from Ystradffin that I saw in my headlights up ahead that a car, Doctor Jones' car, had gone off the road, into the ditch." He paused and took several deep breaths before continuing; "I parked up alongside and got out to see if there was any way in which I could help. The driver's door was lying wide open and there was no one to be seen, although I could tell that something dreadful must have happened. The windscreen was shattered and there seemed to be huge claw marks along the roof of the car and all down the side. As I could see no one, I thought the best thing was to come here and—and, that's when I heard it—" He took another drink.

A great hush had fallen over all of the patrons. They waited with bated breath for Edwin to continue:

"It was a terrible sound that seemed to come from everywhere, yet in the darkness I could see nothing. I'm no hero, so I ran back and got in my car and drove as fast as I could all the way here."

Owen contemplated this new information. He rubbed his chin worriedly. "There's no chance of getting officers out there tonight. In the morning, when my constables arrive, I'll go out and investigate the scene. In the meantime, and certainly in light of what we've all just heard this evening, I think we can safely rule out any involvement on the viscount's part. I would advise everyone to return home, in groups of at least three if possible, and make sure that all their doors are firmly bolted."

* * * * * * *

A cold, damp fog hung like a thick blanket over the area, making driving difficult and hazardous, yet slowly and steadily Owen drove out towards the place Edwin had informed him of the previous night. In the passenger seat sat Constable Hughes, a crudely-drawn map in his hands, whilst in the back of the car, staring out of the window, was Constable Jenkins.

"We can't be far away now, sir," said Hughes. "If this map's anything to go by, I'd say we've probably got less than a mile to go. Just keep going along this road."

"If you want my opinion," butted in Jenkins, "I still think that this Ravenwood sounds a bit of a dodgy character. You said yourself, sir, that he's got a huge dog. Could be that he's trained it to kill people like in that story."

"You mean the Hound of the Baskervilles?" Hughes

laughed, although there was little mirth in it, for they had now ventured far from the village. The realisation that they would shortly be conducting a search of a possible crime scene, one for which the perpetrator or perpetrators responsible remained both unknown and at large, was not something to laugh at. The thought chilled him somewhat.

Owen shifted gear and slowed down, gradually bringing the car to a halt. "We'll walk from here. Keep your eyes peeled for anything out of the ordinary." He got out of the car and put his hand up to his forehead. There was a filming of sweat on it and he felt suddenly cold. Even with the others there, close beside him, he felt oddly afraid. It was nothing he could put his finger on, nothing really tangible, but walking down that barely visible stretch of country road, he had the sudden impression that red eyes were watching his movements with a raptorial hunger. Savagely, he bit his lower lip to prevent himself from screaming out loud. The fear was palpable, clinging around him, soaking into his mind. He stood quite still, listening for a moment, certain that something—some hideous evil—would emerge from the fog and tear them all to pieces.

"Sure is one hell of a creepy place," said Hughes. In the distance, he could hear the bleating of sheep.

"And this fog doesn't help either." Jenkins was walking slowly, eyes scanning the road below him.

They walked on through the fog for a further five minutes or so before Owen brought them up short. He pointed to the ground. "Look! See those tyre marks?

This is clearly were the car began to skid. It looks as though the driver tried to hit the brakes."

"And what's this?" Jenkins, who had walked over to one side, returned with something long and slender in his right hand.

"What have you found?" asked Owen.

"Why, it's an arrow, sir." Jenkins handed it over. "It was just lying on the road."

Carefully, Owen ran his hand down the relatively thick, smooth pine shaft. The black fletching had obviously been well trimmed, and testing the iron-cast barbed point against his thumb, he was not surprised to find that it was incredibly sharp. His appraisal was interrupted by a call from Hughes.

"The car's just up ahead, sir."

"Keep a good hold of this," said Owen, returning the arrow to his constable. "And good work spotting it."

The two of them jogged up the road to join Hughes, who had clambered down into the relatively shallow ditch and was peering inside the wrecked vehicle.

At first glance, it could have just been a simple accident. A car going off the road in adverse driving conditions was not, in itself, an unusual occurrence. However, it was only as they got closer that they noticed the jagged marks that covered the roof and the nearside. It was as though some creature, a bear for instance, had attacked it. Some gouges went right through the metal.

The driver's door hung wide open, and Owen had to hope that the good doctor had somehow managed to escape and that he was out there somewhere trying to make his way back to civilisation. Much as he wanted to believe this, the state of the car and the terrible sounds Edwin had described seemed to make it unlikely. No, he told himself, there was something far more sinister at work here. With that realisation, he clambered down into the ditch to join Hughes.

"Sure is a bit of a mess," said Hughes. "But there's no blood visible, which is rather surprising."

"Most strange." Owen gave a final look around the interior of the car. He drew himself to his full height and straightened his back. His eyes narrowed to mere slits as he tried to push his vision into the enshrouding fog. That feeling of being watched was strong within him once more, as was the unsettling awareness that there was something out there. Something that could see them, despite the fact that they could not see it. A lump gathered in his throat, but he forced it down. There was a sudden cold clamminess of sweat on his back and an icy chill on his chest. He felt his arms shaking.

"Inspector!"

Jenkins' call made him jump.

"There's another arrow over here. And—and something else. I think you'd better have a look."

* * * * * * *

By early afternoon the fog had lifted somewhat, permitting Owen to drive far more easily than he had that morning. Passing through the gateway that led up towards Dyrysgol Castle he suppressed a shiver of fear and he heard Hughes, who was in the passenger seat, let out a little gasp of uncomprehending bewilderment.

"Looking at this lot, it's no wonder that Jenkins thinks that this viscount is behind everything."

"We've got nothing to go by yet, so let's not be too quick to judge, although I'll agree with you this place sure gives me the creeps."

"I—" Hughes was about to speak, when he suddenly stopped and stared. "I think you'll find that we've got plenty to go by, Inspector. Stop the car and look! Over there to the left."

Owen brought the car to an abrupt halt. "What is it?" he asked tersely. His eyes lit up. "Right, let's go. Leave the talking to me. And don't forget to bring that." He pointed meaningfully at a large black bag, which lay on the back seat. With that, he got out of the car and began to stride purposefully towards the near side of the castle.

Some two hundred yards away, he could see Ravenwood shooting arrows at a large, circular straw target.

"Lord Ravenwood!" he shouted.

Ravenwood turned to look at him, an arrow notched on his bow and ready to be released.

"A moment, if you please." Owen was now getting near and the sudden, dreadful thought that he presented a good target to an experienced archer flashed briefly through his mind. He dispelled it the moment Ravenwood lowered his bow and stood waiting, expectantly.

"Inspector. Once again I have the pleasure of your company." Ravenwood stood tall and imposing, the bow he gripped slightly longer than him. "You catch me pursuing one of my great hobbies. As a toxophilite—"

"A what?"

"A toxophilite—a lover of archery. I don't suppose you're aware that the so-called English longbow was in fact invented here, in Wales."

"Is that right? Well that's one of the main reasons why I'm here. You see, two arrows were found at the scene of one of our investigations this morning, and, they seem to be identical in appearance to the ones in your quiver. Now, I had merely come out here on the off chance that perhaps you could have told me something about them, what with your interest in old weapons and such. But here I find you with arrows, very similar in appearance, in your possession. Would you care to explain?"

Hughes had now approached. He opened the bag that he carried and took out the two arrows in question. He gave a slightly mocking look to the viscount that seemed to imply that it was all over for him now. They had the evidence to pin him to one of the disappearances. It would of course be interesting to discover how the man explained the other thing in the bag, but this was, nonetheless, a major breakthrough.

Ravenwood shrugged his shoulders. There was no obvious admission of guilt in his body movement nor in his eyes, only a confirmation that what the other held in his hand did indeed belong to him.

"They are yours, yes?" Owen looked at him with a hard stare.

"Yes, I do believe that they are. And I suppose as a token of my appreciation for your returning them to me, you would like me to explain why they were found where they were, yes?" For the briefest of moments, something almost akin to concern flashed across Ravenwood's fine features. There was no turning back now, he thought to himself. He would have to explain everything and hope that they believed his story. "Shall we go inside, gentlemen?" he said. "I'll have Franklins prepare a little something to eat, and we'll get down to business. There's much to tell."

* * * * * * *

After they had settled themselves in the study and Franklins had made some sandwiches and some tea and coffee, Owen gestured to his constable to open the bag once more. At arms length, as though reluctant to handle whatever it was that had been contained inside, Hughes removed a leathery flap of greyish-black material. What looked like green veins spread out web-like inside it.

"In addition to the arrows, we found this rather repulsive-looking thing. Have you any idea what it is?"

Ravenwood grinned. "I know exactly what it is. However—you may not believe me if I tell you. You see, what you have there is a piece of wyvern wing."

"*What?*" asked the two policemen in unison.

"It's a piece of wyvern wing," Ravenwood repeated. Noting the confusion on the others' faces, he decided that further information was warranted. "The wyvern is a monster. A creature long thought mythological and relegated to the realm of folklore. It's similar in several ways to a dragon and has often been mistaken for one. It has but two legs and it also possesses a fearsome, poisonous barbed sting on the end of its tail. Legend states that the venom kills almost instantly and there is no known antidote. You will find its image displayed on countless shields within this very castle, and indeed, it is the old national emblem of Wales."

Owen and Hughes exchanged disbelieving looks.

"It's this monster which is terrorising Dyrysgol. I should know, for not only have I seen it, but—but it is my duty in life to slay it. I was there yesterday evening, when it attacked the doctor. Alas, I was unable to save him."

"Can I stop you there?" Owen raised an interjecting hand. "Lord Ravenwood, please forgive me if I sound a little brusque, but try and see this from where we're sitting. Wouldn't you agree that what you're saying sounds more than a trifle *odd*? I mean, do you fully expect us to believe that there's a winged monster flying around out there, snatching people up and devouring them?"

"That's exactly what I'm saying, Inspector." There was an intensity in the man's eyes. "And more will fall victim to it, unless we, or rather I, stop it."

"And just assuming that this thing does exist, where can it be found?" inquired Hughes, his question asked without much true interest. He reached for one of the sandwiches and began to munch into it. In his mind, at least, the viscount was stark raving mad. But why not humour the man for a moment? Besides, he was enjoying the sandwiches.

Ravenwood pondered this question for a moment. "Unfortunately, I don't know. Don't you think that if I did, I would have tried to kill it before now?" He put down his coffee cup. "There are a few locations that I have yet to explore. But to tell you the truth, it could be virtually anywhere. It will have laired itself somewhere secluded. Somewhere where it can hide and rest, only coming out on the nights around the full moon to hunt and kill its prey."

"I'm sorry, but I'm still finding all of this very hard to believe," said Owen. "You talk about a monster straight out of the Dark Ages, and expect us to join you on some dragon-slaying mission as though this were normal. *It's not normal*, Lord Ravenwood. It's preposterous. Now, if you'd said there was an escaped bear from a travelling circus on the loose—"

"You have a piece of wing."

"This could be anything," retorted Hughes. "I'll admit I don't know what it is, but I sure as hell don't think that it's part of any dragon." He sneered derisively and looked at his Inspector.

"I told you, it's not a dragon."

"No, it's a wyvern. Isn't that right, Lord Ravenwood?"

There was a tone of contempt and mockery now in Owen's voice. Things were becoming farcical. He was a detective inspector, with a trained, rational mind. He did not believe in the existence of things that he could not see or detect, or understand for that matter. "You'll be telling me next that the thing is immune to bullets or something, won't you?"

"That's correct. Like many creatures of the night, it's impervious to most forms of modern weaponry."

"Ah, hence the archery and the sword-fighting. Yes, I'm beginning to see now."

"Inspector, it's clear that not only are you trying to ridicule me, but that you don't believe a word I'm telling you. It's also clear that you'll soon charge me on some grounds or other in connection with the disappearances. After all, you now have proof to link me incontrovertibly with one of the crime scenes. This leaves me with no alternative but to show you something that I have taken great steps to conceal from the outside world ever since I inherited the castle." Ravenwood rose from his chair. "If you'll follow me."

The two policemen got up and followed Ravenwood as he led them out of the study, back along the main corridor into the hall and then down a further passage which headed deeper into the castle. It was as they were following him, that Owen began to realise the immensity of the building, with its labyrinthine turns and twists, and countless doors leading to an unknown number of rooms. Many of the walls were decorated with paintings and portraits of dour-faced individuals, who stared out at them, sinisterly.

Eventually they arrived at what looked like an old dungeon door.

Removing a key from his pocket, the viscount inserted it into the lock and turned it. There was an audible click and he pushed the door wide, revealing a set of very old steps, worn deeply with age, which led down into what appeared, at first sight, to be a dank cellar from which several other subterranean passages radiated. Taking a torch, which hung on the wall, he switched it on and proceeded down. At the bottom, he took the tunnel on his left. It sloped down steeply.

Their dark shadows flitted ghost-like over the walls as they ventured deeper into the bowels of the castle. Owen was feeling uneasy, claustrophobic, in the dank dungeons. There was an eerie feel, an oddness that soaked into his being, surging along the nerves and fibres of his body. Silence screamed at him and his mind screamed silently in return. His inner sense was telling him to flee from this place, to turn around and run, back up the steps, to the relative safety of the ground floor. Anything could lurk down here in the shadows, he thought.

"I hope there's a damned good reason for bringing us down here, Ravenwood," said Hughes. "This place gives me the creeps."

"Nearly there. Just down this final flight of steps."

The steps in question were, if anything, even more worn and dangerous than those to the entrance to the dungeon, and on two occasions it was only by sheer luck that Owen did not fall headlong down them. They gathered at the bottom and the two policemen stared, slack-jawed at the sight before them.

Illuminated in the torchlight, almost dominating the vaulted chamber they had entered, lay the skeletal, and indeed partially fossilised, remains of some prehistoric monster. Although it was difficult at first to ascertain its true outline amidst the jumble of yellow-aged bones, it was clear that this was no ordinary creature. Its sheer size alone ruled that out as a possibility.

Shaking his head in stunned disbelief, Owen half-stumbled forward on legs that had become leaden. This was amazing! Unreal! He tried to shake the image before him from his perplexed eyes, as though it were nothing more than an illusion brought on by stress and exhaustion. He gripped his hands tightly together, feeling all reality, every trace and last vestige of sanity, crumbling away beneath his feet, dropping away from under him like an avalanche of hard facts and nightmare. He searched his mind frantically, madly, for a rational explanation. Something for his spinning mind to hold onto, an anchor to steady himself.

"Look at those teeth." Hughes had now taken the torch from Ravenwood and was shining the beam directly at the monstrous skull, which rested atop a vertebrae-ridged spine, the neck longer than any giraffe's. He trailed the beam of the torch down, taking in every detail, every bone and protrusion. "And those claws. Good God!"

"This, gentleman, is the remains of the first wyvern.

It has lain here for over thirteen hundred years, ever since my ancestor, the first of the Ravenwoods, slew it. Since that time, it has always been the duty—and to some extent the curse—of the Ravenwoods, to kill it. I've done years of research on the subject, and I now know the secret behind its existence. Whenever a male heir of the Ravenwood line reaches the age of forty, a new wyvern will hatch, spreading fear and horror until it is killed. It's one of the reasons why I've never married. Hopefully when my line dies out, so will the monster's. The question is, just how are we going to find it?"

A sudden idea came to Owen.

* * * * * * *

Dusk was still an hour or so away, when Owen and Ravenwood saw the two approaching vehicles. That in front was the viscount's car driven by Franklins. Behind it, churning up mud, bounced a large tractor pulling a farmyard trailer.

"Well," said Ravenwood. "I hope to God that this plan of yours works. For not only has it cost me a pretty penny, but more importantly, I don't think there are many more nights that the wyvern will fly before the next full moon. This might be our last night, our last chance to get it before it goes into a month-long hibernation."

"It's as good a plan as any. What with the alternative being a full-scale search of all the possible places where it could hide. This area is riddled with old mine shafts, ruined mills, caves, and goodness knows what else. We could spend a year combing the area and still not find it."

"You may be right." Ravenwood winced at the distinct animal stench that wafted out from the trailer, which had now parked up nearby. From inside, came the sound of bleating sheep. "I hope your men don't mind getting their hands dirty," he said, a wry grin on his face.

* * * * * * *

From the bushes, Owen watched the moon come up from behind the castle; a great skull-white disc that glared down out of the star-strewn heavens like a huge, watching, evil eye witnessing their every move. His heart pounded in his chest and his mouth was dry, and he was afraid.

It was the waiting that was the most terrible part of it; having to sit out there in the long and clinging silence, which seemed to throb in his ears, almost tangibly. He could do nothing to force the fear away, knowing that they were waiting in ambush for something abominable. Something seemed to clamp down upon his brain, allowing the horror and the black fear to rise a little higher, to grow a little stronger, until now he could hardly bear it. He thought grimly of the black thing that hovered somewhere up there in the dark sky, waiting to make its nightmare plunge. But there was nothing there. Nothing moved in the deep pools of ebony shadow. No sound. No movement. Nothing. He breathed in deeply, striving vaguely to still the sudden hammering of his heart and the violent pumping of the blood in his veins.

The stench from the scattered sheep viscera was repugnant, and he felt a little twinge of sympathy for the two remaining live animals which were tethered in its midst. Still, if the bait worked, it will have been worth it, he thought.

He almost jumped when Ravenwood grabbed his shoulder and pointed. He looked up, and there, silhouetted against the moon, he saw it! A chill of utter horror ran down his spine. It clutched at his body with ripping, seeking fingers, and it was only with a great mental effort that he stopped himself from screaming out loud.

The winged monstrosity circled lazily overhead before starting a descent, its twin claws extended. It swooped down like some hellish bird of prey and plucked one of the sheep from the ground before taking to the wing once more.

"We have to try and lure it down," whispered Ravenwood, his longbow in hand. "If we can get it near enough, I will be able to shoot it."

It had clearly devoured the first sheep in mid-flight, for Owen could see that it was now preparing itself for a second dive. This would probably be their last chance. With an insane compulsion, he broke from the cover of the bushes and ran out into the open, waving his hands and shouting at the top of his voice.

Hellish, lambent red eyes fixed on him from high

above. For a fleeting moment, he was the rabbit in the eyes of the hawk. And then it plummeted towards him, its wings outstretched and membranous, horn-like spurs at their tips.

At that moment, Ravenwood and the two constables charged into the clearing. The viscount launched an arrow, and then a second whilst the policemen discharged their shotguns, which Franklins had purchased from the farmer earlier that day. Caught in the crossfire, the wyvern whirled and spun, its poison-barbed tail lashing at the air and dripping venom.

Owen scrambled clear. "Shoot it! Kill it!" he hollered.

The wyvern landed on its two legs and turned to face Hughes and Jones. It screeched directly at them. Its voice—the voice of the dark and its power over the light—sent a wave of fear through the two constables, for it touched upon the primal fears buried in the marrow of all living creatures. Their knees buckled under them and they fell screaming to the ground, covering their ears with trembling hands. And in that moment, it flapped towards them. Its huge jaws clamped around Hughes and, shaking him from side-to-side, it tossed his headless body away.

It was just about to snap down on Jones, when another arrow struck into its left flank, causing it to spin round and face the advancing archer. A second arrow sunk deep in its chest, drawing a further snarl of rage and anger from it.

Suddenly the terrible carnage was illuminated in ghastly detail as Franklins turned on the headlights of his car and came speeding towards it.

Owen stifled a cry as he saw the reptilian horror turn to face the oncoming vehicle. He felt helpless, unable to intervene, rooted to the spot. Paralysed, all he could do was watch through horror-filled eyes.

And then all hell broke loose! There were cries and shouts and shotguns blasts and that infernal screeching. The wyvern had been wounded, whether from the impact from Franklins' car or from the half dozen or so arrows which now protruded from its bat-like wings, he could not immediately tell. In one terrible moment, he witnessed the manservant's car being overturned and the unfortunate being inside horribly rended by the monster's snatching claws.

With a cry, Ravenwood, now out of arrows, leapt into the fray, swinging his broadsword. Hacking and chopping with abandon, he threw all caution to the wind and set about the beast. With a mighty two-handed swing he completely severed one of the wyvern's wings. A follow-up chop sliced a great gash down its flank. Dark greenish blood spattered.

But then, just as it appeared as though Ravenwood had the upper hand and was about to vanquish the beast, its snake-like tail lashed forward, the barbed stinger striking him in the right thigh. He screamed in agony. In one final, desperate act, with the lethal toxin spreading through his body, he drove his sword through the dragon-like head, silencing the Dyrysgol horror forever.

Stumbling, staggering, Owen lurched forward.

Ravenwood was not quite dead but he could see that there was nothing he could do to save him.

"And so it ends," Ravenwood managed to gasp. "Get rid of the body if you can. Burn it."

"Inspector!" Jones came rushing over, trying not to look at the bloody aftermath of their confrontation. "How in hell's name are we going to explain all this?" he cried manically.

Owen shook his head, unable to take in the reality of what had just transpired. "I—don't know, I really don't know. But hopefully the nightmare is now over." He could see that Viscount Ravenwood was now dead, and he had to hope that with his death Dyrysgol would now be safe.

THE DOLL

Who knew what horrors the doll had seen through the centuries?

"It never ceases to surprise me just how much rubbish someone can collect over the course of a lifetime." Stanley Jones sipped from his cup of tea, surrounded by chests and boxes of various shapes and sizes, most of which had now been packed with antique child's toys; spinning tops, garishly-painted marionettes, hand-crafted wooden animals, small drums, and the like. Faint rays of sunlight shone in through the small attic window, filtering through the thin cloud of dust motes, which were suspended in the musty air.

"Me too," replied Michael Hargreaves. "Although that said, according to Briggs, some of this stuff could well be worth a bob or two." He pointed to a pile of heaped paintings, which rested on a chair nearby. "Take that lot there, for instance. Although they may look a bit tatty, and I for one don't like the look of them, I daresay someone will pay through the nose for them at the auction."

Jones finished his tea, got up from his chair, and walked over to examine the paintings. Removing a rag from a pocket in his brown overalls, he reached down and wiped free the layer of dust which had accumulated on the topmost painting. It was an old-fashion oil painting, a landscape, featuring a majestic yet dark and foreboding castle set atop a densely-wooded mountain. The thunderous brooding skies augmented its sinister appearance.

"What do you think?" asked Hargreaves, getting up and walking over.

"I'm just seeing if I can find a signature." Jones rubbed his rag around the edge of the painting and then along the ornately-carved frame. "Doesn't seem to be any."

"Still hoping to find a long-lost da Vinci?"

"I'd be so lucky." Jones returned his rag to his pocket. "How long have we now been in this business? Ten, eleven years? You would have thought in all those years of clearing out some of these old houses, we would have come across something of value. The one and only time I ever found something of any real worth was that Edwardian chest of drawers—"

"The one from the old Fitzwilliam place? I remember. Didn't one of the heirs turn up to claim it or something?"

"That's right. Beats me how he hadn't learned of the old man's demise earlier. After all, his obituary had been in all of the papers. Besides, Briggs is usually very thorough checking up on whether or not there are any living next of kin." Jones removed a packet of cigarettes from his pocket.

Hargreaves leaned forward and accepted the cigarette the other offered. He inhaled it quickly into lighting, then scowled down at it, rolling it absently between his fingers. "You know, there are times when I've been tempted to pocket a little something or other. After all, it's not really like stealing, is it? I mean, who's going to miss the odd necklace or a few rings? It's not as if the old man who lived here kept an inventory of all his worldly possessions, now is it? And as you said yourself, some of this might fetch a—" He stopped abruptly upon hearing the sounds of a door slamming downstairs and the sound of heavy footsteps coming closer.

They glanced guiltily at each other and tried to look busy.

A few seconds later the door to the small attic room was flung open and Peter Briggs stepped inside. He was a short, slightly fat man in his late fifties; balding and bespectacled, his forehead wrinkled by worry frowns. In his right hand he held a clipboard, and he carried about him an air of officiousness.

Jones stubbed out his cigarette and jumped to attention. "We're getting there, boss," he said. "This is the last room in the house. We've packed up all of the pieces from the two large rooms downstairs, and we've got most of the furniture outside waiting for the delivery van. It was a struggle getting that piano down from the upstairs bedroom, but we managed it."

Stepping further into the room, Briggs flung his disapproving look around the cluttered attic room. He ran the fingers of his right hand over a thick layer of dust on one of the nearby crates before looking at both of his workmen. "I want all of this lot out of here by this evening. Do you think you can do that?"

"I think we can manage that, boss," answered Jones. He indicated to where an array of unsorted clutter lay scattered haphazardly in the far corner of the room: the iron frame of a child's bed, a broken rocking-horse, several small chairs, and other miscellaneous pieces of dated furniture. "It's just a case of getting that lot packed and then shifting what's up here outside."

"Well then, jump to it," said Briggs. "The sooner we've done this house clearance, the better. There's something about this place that just doesn't feel right."

There was something in the way that his foreman had made this declaration that made Hargreaves uneasy. It was an admittance of what he himself had been feeling for the past week ever since he had set foot in the old house. Although as a level-headed, practical man, it was something he had not dared confide to any of the others. Now, after what Briggs had said, he thought it was time to raise certain issues.

"You're not the only one who thinks there's something not quite right going on here," he said.

"What's that?" asked Briggs. He looked up at Hargreaves.

"Well, it's just that I too have had the feeling that there's something, what shall I say, slightly spooky going on here. It's not something I've mentioned before for fear that either of you would think that I'm beginning to lose my marbles or something." Hargreaves looked to Jones for some kind of support, but saw only blankness in his weary-looking face before continuing: "It's worse up here in the attic. At times, when I've been up here on my own, I, well—"

"Well, what?" inquired Briggs. "Let's hear it, then."

Hargreaves looked uncomfortable. He bit his lower lip and ran a hand through his thinning hair. He looked down at his scuffed shoes for a moment before looking up. He swallowed a lump in his throat. "I'm sure I've heard the sound of a child whimpering, crying almost. It's very faint, and I'm not sure if it's just the sound of the wind blowing through the eaves or what, but it sure has scared the hell out of me. I don't know about either of you, but I also get the feeling that it's much colder up here than it is downstairs. Don't you feel it?"

A little chill shivered down Brigg's spine, and he felt a sudden nervous tenseness shudder through his whole body, forming a tight knot of fear in his stomach. He had worked in the removal and acquisition business for over thirty years, and had been in countless houses, private homes, and mansions across the country throughout his career, and he had to admit there had been a few instances when the fearful realisation that he was handling the treasures and personal effects of the recently deceased had made him distinctly uneasy. At such times, he had had to wrestle hard with his own conscience to dismiss the belief that what he was making a living from could be viewed by some as nothing more than legalised grave-robbing. It was undeniable that there was a certain ghoulish element to the entire business.

"*I* don't feel anything. I think this is just a load of nonsense." In an act of purposefulness, Jones put on his workmen's gloves. "The sooner we get this stuff into crates and get it outside, the sooner the job will be done. I'll admit there is some weird stuff here, but I don't believe in ghosts. Never have. Never will."

"I bet you would if something were to walk through that wall over there," said Briggs, trying to a inject a little joviality into a topic which was becoming increasingly macabre. He pointed to a portion of wall close to the old bricked-up fireplace. "I must say, when I first came up here, a few days ago, I half-expected to find a coffin or two up here."

"I'd rather you didn't talk like that," complained Hargreaves. "This place gives me the creeps enough as it is. He must have been a bit of a weird one to have lived here all alone. And that raises another thing—why would an old man, whom you've already told us had no family, have child's toys and things up here?"

"Beats me." Briggs consulted his clipboard. "According to all the details, Mr. von Shaffer was to all extents and purposes a bit of a hoarder. It could be that he collected some of these things. Though why he would want to stick them all up here in this room, away from everything else, is a bit of a mystery. A bit like the man himself. From what little I've pieced together, it would appear that he came over from Germany or Austria sometime during the reign of

Victoria, although I've been unable to ascertain any true records pertaining to him. Consequently, I've been unable to track down any surviving relatives who may be entitled to a share of some of his possessions. Similarly, like so many foreigners, he left no will, no one to whom he bequeathed any of this." He gave an encompassing wave of his hand. "Anyhow, it looks as though you're nearly done up here. We'll get that lot in the corner cleared out, and I'll put it all down in the inventory and then we'll get it packed up and—" He shivered uncontrollably as the almost undetectable sound of a child crying emanated from the far corner before being cut abruptly short. Eyes wide, he stood stock still.

"Did you hear that?" hissed Hargreaves, staring wildly.

"Hear what?" Following the other's gaze, Jones glanced around. There was nothing out of the ordinary. No headless wraiths materialising out of the floorboards, or hideous, fanged corpse-faces at the window.

"It was—only the wind," said Briggs, uncertainly. His face had gone several tones paler. Relax, he told himself, relax. The idea that anything could be wrong was utterly ludicrous, totally ridiculous. He felt a little tremor of fear pass through him. It was almost as if there was something—some presence—in the room with them. And that whatever it was, it had neither shape nor substance. Rather, it was a feeling, an impression of looming malevolence that touched his mind with a finger of ice. Thoughts clashed inside his head, and he felt the sudden deathly silence pull at him. He tried to steady himself. "Come on, let's hurry this up. The sooner we get this done, the sooner we'll be away from here."

"Right you are, boss." Oblivious to the nervous actions of his companions, Jones started towards the untidy heap of child's toys and furniture that had been tucked away in the shadowy corner of the attic room. The wooden boards of the floor creaked under his heavy feet and a sprinkling of dust fell from the raftered ceiling.

Reluctantly, Hargreaves walked over to assist. They soon got their usual working rhythm going, with Jones clearing the bric-a-brac and handing it to the other, who would then take it over to Briggs. It was then the foreman's duty to record a reasonable description and assessment of the item before it was finally packed up. And, whereas Jones worked with a cold efficiency, the other two men were edgy, occasionally stopping to look and listen, straining their senses for the undetectable.

There were no repeats of the eerie sound that had scared them earlier, and, after half an hour, they had managed to clear away and log everything, with only the iron framework of the child's bed remaining. In a somewhat cavalier attitude, Jones reached down and hauled it to one side, the metal legs scraping across the floor. It was a cumbersome piece of furniture, and it took both himself and Hargreaves to manhandle it across the room. In the process of doing so, one of the struts of the framework snagged on Hargreaves's chest, ripping open the front of his overalls and dislodging the pencil he kept in his breast pocket.

With a grunt, he lowered the bed to the floor, walked around Jones and looked down to see where his pencil had gone. It could not be seen, and his first guess was that it had rolled underneath one of the packing crates.

"Are you all right, Mike? That looks like quite a nasty scratch you got there." Jones nodded to where the child's bed had snagged the other.

"Eh?" With some level of surprise, Hargreaves looked at the ragged tear on his chest and saw that a small puddle of blood was spreading on his white undershirt. He put his fingers to the dampness. "It's just a scratch. I think I'll live." He looked down again, eyes searching. "Can't seem to see my pencil. Pass me your torch, will you, and I'll see if it's rolled under one of the crates."

He went down on bended knees and pointed the torch beam to the floor. He traced the line of the narrow beam back and forth, seeing where their footprints had scuffed over the dust-covered floorboards. He went down to almost eye level with the floor and looked under several of the crates. It was as he was about to give up searching, that he saw a small anomaly in the woodwork, an almost imperceptible raised board that clearly signified the presence of a small, cunningly concealed trapdoor. "Stan! Come and have a look at this."

"What is it?" asked Jones, crouching down to get a

better look.

"Looks like some kind of compartment. Get me a screwdriver and I'll try and prise the lid up."

Briggs had now stepped over, intrigued as to what this find might reveal. There had been talk that von Shaffer had been a very wealthy man, and it stood to reason that he could have secreted his personal fortune away somewhere in a place such as this. And Briggs was the kind of man who was not adverse to making a little extra profit if and when the opportunity arose. It would be easy enough to fob his two underlings off with a few pounds, telling them that he was going to turn the remainder over to the state, whereas in reality he would see to it that he was the sole beneficiary. His greedy mind had temporarily forgotten about his unease.

With the use of a screwdriver, Hargreaves succeeded in levering up the square wooden lid. Brushing away a fairly large spider which had crawled out from underneath, he directed the torch beam into the shallow cavity beyond. The light revealed a small, rectangular, leather casket of some description. It was sealed by brass clasps and a peculiar-looking lock.

"Well, get it out," ordered Briggs impatiently, signalling with his hands. "Let's have a look at it."

Gingerly, Hargreaves reached in and lifted it free from the cavity in which it had been deposited. It was not particularly heavy, but as he raised it something inside seemed to shift, almost causing him to drop it in alarm. Hurriedly, he placed it on top of one of the crates.

Briggs cast his appraising eye over the container. It was certainly old. Far older than any of the other things they had already found in the attic. He reckoned it to be older than anything he had ever come across before. The leather was cracked and discoloured in places, the bindings showing signs of rust amongst their intricate designs. There was a strange smell coming from it as well. He ran the tips of the fingers of his right hand across it, wincing inexplicably at the age-old feel.

"Don't ask me why, but I've a bad feeling about this box," Hargreaves said, taking a step or two back from it. "To my mind it's clear that whoever hid it up here do so for a reason. I think this is something that was meant to remain hidden."

"Absolute nonsense," sneered Jones derisively. "It could be filled with doubloons or precious jewellery. It's undoubtedly the safe-box the old man stored his money in. Give me the screwdriver and I'll see if I can get the blasted thing open." With a sudden movement, he snatched the screwdriver out of Hargreaves' hand and thrust it into the narrow dividing line between the box and its lid.

"Just be careful how you handle that thing," admonished Briggs. "The box alone looks like it could be worth several hundred pounds. I've never seen anything quite as intricate or as old as that. It doesn't look British. Probably eastern European."

Wiggling the screwdriver back and forth, Jones slowly began to force the lid up. With a protesting screech of tortured metal the brass clasps broke free. The lock was proving harder to jemmy open and sweat was beginning to pop out on Jones' forehead. "Nearly...there. Just a little—" And then, suddenly, the lid sprang open almost as though whatever lay inside wanted to get out.

Eagerly, the three men gathered around the small leather casket and peered inside.

* * * * * * *

"Ladies and gentlemen, your attention please," said the bald-headed auctioneer from his podium. Pushing his horn-rimmed spectacles back on his head, he glanced down at the small slip of paper, which contained the necessary information regarding the next item. He read from it: "Lot number ninety-seven." He cleared his throat as his assistant, who stood nearby, delicately lifted what at first glance appeared to be a very small child, but was in fact a rather scary-looking doll dressed in a very old and tattered white lace dress.

The assistant held it at arms length as though loath to handle the doll. There was a look of mild disgust on his face. One could have been forgiven for attributing his facial expression to downright fear or revulsion.

Seated towards the rear of the small gathering of antique collectors, Briggs could feel the sweat pop out on his forehead. His hands felt clammy and he shifted uneasily in his chair. He still wasn't sure what compulsion had brought him to the auction.

The auctioneer went on: "What we have here is a

fine example of an early seventeenth-century mid-European doll. No doubt she would have been the prized possession of a young girl of some standing, as can be deduced from the style and the elegance of her clothing. One would like to think she may have even graced the hands of a young countess at sometime in the past. The lot also includes an as yet untranslated diary, probably written by the doll's owner, as well as an accompanying small silver crucifix on a silver chain."

Briggs swallowed a lump in his throat.

"Can we start the bidding at—shall we say, a hundred pounds?" The auctioneer's gaze panned around the seated crowd. For a moment there was nothing but silence. "Very well, can we say eighty pounds?"

Still no interest.

The auctioneer frowned and puckered his lips. It had on the whole been a very slow day, and he himself was not overly fond of the doll, which had sat on display in a cabinet in the auction room for the past ten days; consequently, he was not all that surprised that no one seemed to want it. It had filled him with a sense of unease whenever he had been close to it, and he would be glad to be rid of it, for a sensible price at least. "Seventy pounds, then. Sixty-five?"

"*I* will purchase the doll for sixty pounds."

Heads turned around in the auction hall, and the auctioneer shifted his gaze to the tall, gaunt figure stood to one side. He was dressed in a long black raincoat and his accent was clearly not English, German perhaps.

Briggs eyed the stranger intently, noting what appeared to be a leering smile of triumph on his lean features and a mocking glint in his close-set eyes. For some inexplicable reason, he suddenly had the compulsive thought that it would be dangerous for the doll to fall into the hands of this man. Without fully knowing why, he raised his hand and said: "Seventy."

Without a moment's hesitation, the rain-coated man riposted: "Eighty."

Briggs threw him a swift, disapproving glance. A little muscle was beginning to twitch uncontrollably in his left cheek, as a little imp of apprehension began to nag at his innermost thoughts. There was clearly something he found disturbing about the other individual who he had not noticed previously in the auction hall. It was as though he had just mysteriously arrived for that one lot only.

"It would appear that we have finally got some interest in this antique piece," announced the auctioneer. "Are there any advances on eighty pounds?" His eyes flicked around the seated crowd. He reached for his gavel. "Going once—"

"Ninety pounds," blurted Briggs. It was more than he could afford, but the compulsion to ensure that the doll did not go into the other's keep compelled him to make the offer.

"One hundred," came the stranger's cold, accented reply as a muttered hush went through the auction hall. It was clear that some of the other bargain hunters and antique collectors had now gotten wind of the possibility that the doll was far more valuable than their previous assessments had ascertained. It was not unusual for two seasoned bidders to compete against one another if they were privy to specialised knowledge regarding the true worth of a given piece.

"One hundred and ten!" rang out a woman's voice from the front row. Someone new had now entered the bidding arena.

Hope for a good outcome sprung in the auctioneer. He would not be surprised if this developed into a full-blown bidding war, and in which case the doll could well reach something in the region of two hundred pounds. His shock was visible when, the tall, thin man with the raincoat said rather nonchalantly:

"In order to speed up the inevitable, I will purchase the doll for five hundred pounds."

A great murmuring came from the gathered crowd. This was something none of them had anticipated. It was completely unheard of. Five hundred pounds for an old doll, a tatty notebook containing an untranslated account, and a small silver crucifix!

Briggs' eyes narrowed. There was something mighty suspicious going on here; something that he felt he had to get to the bottom of. Was it possible that the man who had just made the astonishing bid was a friend or indeed relative of von Shaffer, the old man in whose house the doll had been found? With that thought going through his head, he was only dimly aware of the auctioneer bringing down his gavel to seal the bid.

* * * * * * *

Later that afternoon, Briggs sat behind his desk finishing off some paperwork. There was still quite a lot of cataloguing to do regarding the von Shaffer property. Although most had been auctioned off, albeit at a slight loss, there had been sufficient interest in some of the general paintings and objets d'art to have made it quite worthwhile. Then, of course, there had also been the doll, the sale of which had played strongly on his mind.

There had to be more to it. It did not stand to reason that someone would pay such a price for something, which at face value at least, was rather inferior. After all, it was just a doll. The small diary—if indeed that is what it was—would not fetch much, and the tiny silver crucifix which had on first discovery been found draped over the doll's head could be worth no more than twenty pounds at current prices. So why had the foreigner been willing to pay whatever sum was required in order to procure the doll?

Determination overcame Briggs. He had to find out more. He had to.

Consulting his small notebook, he found the phone number for the auction hall and made the call. After four rings the phone on the other side was picked up.

"Reids' auction house. How can I help you?"

"Is that you, Malcolm? It's Briggs here."

"Good afternoon, Mr. Briggs. A fairly good morning's work, wouldn't you say?"

"Yes, yes. I'm enquiring after one of the lots from

the von Shaffer sale—"

"The doll, by chance?" interrupted the other.

"Yes, the doll. I realise that it's rather an unusual question, but do you by chance have any information on the buyer? Name, address, nationality?"

There was a moment's pause. Then: "You don't think there's anything fishy going on do you?" asked the auctioneer. "The gentleman in question did seem a trifle odd, and I've never seen him at any of the auctions here before, although, that said, young Harvey, my assistant, said that he'd seen him looking through the accompanying diary on two occasions. Regardless, he did pay good money, and it was clear that he had his heart set on owning the doll. Heavens knows why, for I found it rather—creepy—if I do say so myself."

"Creepy?" A cold shiver went through Briggs. For some terrible reason he felt the sudden urge to look over his shoulder to ensure that the doll was not crawling its way across the carpet towards him.

"Well, you know what it's like. Certain objects can instil a sense of general unease, I suppose. It was something about the doll's face, I guess. Like some of those old portraits where the eyes seem to follow you around the room no matter where you go. There was also a small cross-shaped burn in the dress, which I don't suppose you noticed. At first, I thought it might have been a reaction of the silver from the crucifix oxidising onto the fabric of the dress. Had we been able to analyse this under a microscope, we would have been able to find out for sure. To my eye, believe it or not, it looked more like a burn mark. Anyway, it's someone else's now. Although I don't know why it should have fetched so much."

"That's exactly what I'm trying to find out. Any information you can provide would be kept in the strictest confidence, of course."

"Hmm. It is against all regulations and company policy."

"Please, Malcolm. You help me out with this one, and I'll see that your company gets a bigger share of the proceeds from our next house clearance."

There came a resigned sigh from the other side of the phone. "Very well, Mr. Briggs. Bear with me for a minute or two while I get the necessary documentation."

Briggs removed a pen from a draw and waited.

After a few minutes break, the phone was picked up again. "Here we are. All right, Mr. Briggs, here are the details you seek. The buyer was a Mr. Lagur Thorko." He spelled the name out to the other. "A Hungarian collector of antiquities. The address given is number one hundred and nineteen Warwick Close, here in the city. No phone number."

Briggs jotted down the details. "I appreciate your assistance, Malcolm."

"Yes, well, let's not make a habit of prying into private buyers' details, shall we? Oh, by the way, just on the off chance you're going out to see him, you might want to swing round to the auction hall first."

"Why's that?" asked Briggs.

"Well it would appear that in his haste to get away with his new acquisition, he forgot to take the little silver crucifix with him. If you were to deliver it, it would save me from having to do so."

* * * * * * *

It was raining heavily and the sky was dark as Briggs turned his car into Warwick Close. The tall houses on either side appeared abandoned, and some of them showed signs of great decrepitude, with missing slates and broken or boarded-up windows featuring predominantly. No lights could be seen in any of the windows, and he had seen no other cars or pedestrians for about the past five minutes, leading him to the belief that this part of the city was shunned for some reason or another. Why anyone who could afford to pay five hundred pounds for a ghastly-looking antique doll would desire to take up residence in such a rundown district was beyond him. It didn't seem right at all.

He strained his eyes in order to discern the house numbers that were barely visible on his right-hand side. The houses seemed to increase in their level of general dilapidation the further he went. He had lived in the city all of his life, and had fortunately never been aware of this part before. It would come as no surprise to find that no one lived here any more.

Passing a small and obviously long-forgotten and clearly neglected cemetery on his left, its outer boundary delineated by a length of spiked iron railing, he soon drew up outside number one hundred and nineteen. From the car window he peered up at the rambling house. Straining his eyes, he could make out what appeared to be flickering candlelight in one of the upstairs rooms.

He opened the door of his car and stepped out. He shivered, plucking at the lapels of his raincoat, feeling the rain soaking through the thin cloth. Completely isolated, standing in a part of the city that was completely foreign to him, he felt very insecure and frightened, mentally debating with himself whether or not he had made a wise judgement in venturing out here alone. Would it not have been better had he come accompanied by either Hargreaves or Jones, or perhaps even Malcolm Reid, the auctioneer, for that matter?

Desperately, he tried to pull himself together. What was the damn matter with him anyway? He had a valid reason to be there—to return some of the buyer's property, and perhaps he could find an explanation for the unease he had felt since he had first set eyes on the doll. Instinctively, the fingers of his right hand clenched around the small silver crucifix in his pocket.

He reached the tall iron gates of the house. For a long moment he stood hesitant, swaying against the growing wind, peering at the gloomy structure with its turreted towers, probing at the darkening sky. It would be easy, he thought, for a house such as this to earn a reputation for being haunted. All it would take would be for a person to see this place as he now saw it, with the witch's moon now climbing up behind the rearing outer walls, and that strange, eerie light coming from the upper window.

He began to hope that the owner would not be in; that being the case, he would rapidly get back into his car and drive home, along sanely-lit streets inhabited by normal, living people. Yet, an unsettling notion in his brain told him there *was* someone in, and that that *someone* was even now spying on him from a darkened window, watching his every move, deliberating on the purpose of his visit.

Mustering up his courage, Briggs pushed open the gates and walked up the short drive to the front door. He reached out a hand to knock, then drew it back sharply as it swung open on noiseless hinges, revealing the yawning blackness of the entrance. His heart contracted rapidly for a moment, and he could hear the blood pounding in his ears. Then he sucked in a deep breath, fingered the little crucifix in his pocket for assurance, and stepped through into the interior of the house. Now that he was inside, he saw that there was, indeed, a faint glow coming from the top of the stairs directly in front of him. The house smelled of age-old dust, rising damp, and neglect, smells which, due to his profession, he was quite acquainted with.

On the landing above, a shadowy figure appeared, silhouetted against the candlelight, the eldritch glow at his back like an unholy halo about him.

"Good evening."

Briggs felt his heart leap. For a moment it felt as though his throat had dried up completely and that he had lost the power of speech. He swayed on his feet, and the feeling that the man's voice held a slightly hypnotic quality dulled his mind for a moment, blanking out any other thoughts. It had sounded cold yet mellow.

The tall figure began to descend the stairs, his cast shadow unnaturally long and menacing.

With a strong conscious effort, Briggs shook his head free of the strange spell the other had on him. "Mr. Thorko, I—I'd like to introduce myself. My name is Peter Briggs, and I've—"

"You've come to return something of mine? I knew you would." Thorko was nearly at the bottom of the stairs now, and in the shadowy light from above, his features looked even more cadaverous than they had when Briggs had first seen him. He was dressed in a relatively well-tailored dark suit that, combined with his macabre demeanour and appearance, did little to calm Briggs' nerves. The man could have just stepped from a coffin or a funeral parlour.

I knew you would, Briggs didn't like the sound of that. Nervously, he gently chewed his lower lip. He was trembling slightly. Somehow, he found the strength of will to reply: "Yes, that's right." His fingers tightened around the crucifix in his pocket. Although he had never been a believer in the existence of vampires, he was half-expecting the man before him with the central European accent to suddenly sprout fangs and leap at him or else turn into a bat. But that's preposterous, he told himself fiercely, trying to shake away the frightening thoughts. He removed the crucifix on its little chain from his pocket and held it out on his upturned palm.

Although he had expected the other to suddenly recoil from the sight of it, he was pleasantly surprised to note just a flicker of indifference in the other's eyes.

"To tell you the truth, Mr. Briggs, I did not forget it. I merely chose not to take it." Something diabolical and malignant glinted in the other's dark eyes. "You see, I have no need of it. Now that I have her, such trinkets are no longer necessary. You may dispose of it as you see fit."

Her? Was he referring to the doll? Briggs stared at him uncertainly. He was about to say something when suddenly the door behind him swung shut.

A cruel smile creased itself into being on Thorko's face. It was not a pleasant sight.

"What the devil's going on here?" shouted Briggs. He turned towards the door and tried the handle. It was locked!

"Now there's a question," demurred Thorko, "and one which I think should be answered. After all, you're going to play a significant part in tonight's activities. But first—"

"Not likely." Briggs flung his weight at the door. It pained his shoulder but did not budge. He turned. "Now, I'm telling you—"

"*You're* telling me?" Thorko's eyes flared a deep crimson.

The strength seemed to sap from Briggs' limbs, and he had to steady himself against a wall to prevent himself from collapsing as his left knee buckled under him. Dark thoughts pervaded his mind, and he felt as though he was falling through a swirling red mist, filled with unseen, yet horrible creatures. There was the faint sounds of people screaming, of people being sadistically tortured and killed. Gritting his teeth, he somehow managed to hold on to some vestige of sanity, and he was vaguely aware that the other was guiding him, effortlessly, slowly upstairs towards that dimly-lit room from which the candlelight emanated.

The other was talking, the words barely heard: "Had you taken the time to study my notebook, and had you been able to read Old Hungarian, you might have saved yourself a lot of trouble, Mr. Briggs. You see, *I* wrote that a long time ago. In the late summer of 1614, to be exact."

They were near the landing now, and Briggs felt as though he had been drugged or something. He was struggling to keep his eyes open.

"I remember well my dungeon study in Csejthe Castle, where I would instruct my countess and her dark sisters in Black Magic. Elizabeth had been such an apt and willing student, eager to embrace all that I could teach."

They were now at the door to the candlelit room.

Briggs felt bile rise to his throat. Somehow, he had to fight against this draining, compelling authority, which the other seemed to have over him. His will was fading fast. Through eyes that could hardly comprehend what they were seeing, he stared forward as Thorko steered him into the room. It was almost as though he was seeing with his mind's eye, as opposed to his natural vision. The scene before him distorted and wavered.

A ghastly, hellish glow had suffused the entire room from some source near the ceiling. A crazy pattern had been painted on the smooth wooden floorboards, and a great carved altar had been installed at the far end of the room. Over it hung a grotesque, snake-like monstrosity crushing an inverted cross in its awesome coils.

Through weakened vision, Briggs could see the small shape of the doll lying in the centre of the peculiar markings on the floor.

"For too long she has been lost, buried away in secret places by those who sought to contain her. But now her time will come again, Mr. Briggs, and I will see her returned to her ancestral lands." Thorko stretched an almost skeletal hand out to where the doll lay. "My lady, Countess Bathory. In the final days as she was confined to her quarters and her sisters in witchcraft, Dorottya and Darvulia Szenter and Erzi Majorva were burnt at the stake, I managed to fashion the doll from one of her favourite playthings, in which I could contain her soul. Through the blood of countless virgins, she had managed to prolong her youthful appearance, but it was only I who could ensure that she survived her imprisonment. Starved of the means to prolong her life, she pleaded with me so that I could ensure her revenge. Once your blood is offered to her, she will awaken and bathe in the blood of many once more."

Reason and clarity tried in vain to come to the fore

within Briggs' mind. This was impossible. It defied all that he had ever believed in. How could this be real? It was a nightmare. One from which he had to wake, and soon.

He was being dragged, slowly and yet with a strength of devilish purposefulness, towards the altar. Atop which he could see a large sacrificial knife and a goblet of pure silver. He tried to scream out loud, but his cry was reduced to nothing more than a whimpering sigh as he saw Thorko now standing over him, the glinting weapon held aloft...

* * * * * * *

Ron Sturgess and John Wilson entered the small room at the top of the narrow flight of stairs. It was cramped and dingy, and there was a peculiar odour, a repugnant stench, emanating from somewhere. What visible furniture they could see was either torn or broken, and a few rats scampered away in all directions.

"What a tip," commented Sturgess, kicking aside an overturned chair. "Why is it we always find the worst rooms are at the top? It's as though this place has been used as a communal junkyard."

"What I find more surprising," added Wilson, "is the fact that some property developer reckons he can make a go of these old buildings. I guess he'll probably knock most of them down and then rebuild. That would make some sense, I guess."

Sturgess sniffed at the foul air. "Phew. It certainly

stinks. You'd think that something died up here."

"Could be that something did," commented Wilson with a wry grin. "If my memory serves me right, it was in one of these houses, maybe the very one we're in, that some fella was supposed to have vanished some three years ago. He too was in the removal business, I seem to recall. Or maybe it was something to do with reclaiming old property? Anyhow, I seem to think it was old Malcolm Reid, the auctioneer, who informed the police that this is where the missing man had last gone."

Sturgess raised an eyebrow. "You're joking, right?" he asked out of morbid curiosity.

"No. I remember reading about it in the papers. The police came out, but couldn't find anything. Not a trace." Wilson advanced further into the small attic room, assessing just how much work would be involved with clearing all of the visible junk. "The house had been rented by some Bulgarian, but by the time the police had come to question him he had fled the country. They put out a photograph of him along with his daughter taken at the airport, but somehow they managed to get out of the country. One rumour had it that there was some suspicion of espionage what with the Eastern bloc connection. Something to do with a doll which may've had top secret documents hidden in it."

"Sounds dodgy to me." Sturgess wasn't that interested. He struggled his way through the obstacle of heaped furniture towards the back of the room.

"Anyhow, I reckon we've certainly got our work cut out getting this lot downstairs and outside. I reckon it's going to be at least a day's work." Ungainly, he clambered over the remains of an old bed in order to get at the wardrobe that stood leaning against the far wall. He turned to his workmate. "The stink's worse from over here. Hell! Just imagine if his dead body's inside."

Wilson gave a grim smile. "Well, are you going to open it?"

Sturgess pondered the question for a moment or two, uncertainty rising within him. Then, marshalling his courage, he stepped to one side and opened the wardrobe door. It was with some relief that no corpse fell out from it. "Hah!" he laughed harshly. "There's nothing but old coats." It was only as he took a step back that his right foot contacted with a loose floorboard causing it to swing up. In shocked surprise, he glanced down at the space beneath it, and saw with mind-numbing horror the desiccated and rat-gnawed face of the late Peter Briggs staring up at him. From what remained of his mouth protruded a length of fine silver chain.

THE STUFF OF
NIGHTMARES

*Every night the clown came back, creeping
slowly up the stairs and into Dixon's room.*

Doctor John Fordham frowned, a perplexed and
frustrated look on his face. "Mr. Dixon." He briefly
consulted his notebook. "This is now your fourth
visit. And yet, despite our ongoing therapy sessions
I'm afraid you don't seem to be making much, if any,
progress. I've told you repeatedly that all these fears
that you're displaying are purely imaginary. You suffer
from purely delusional symptoms, which, of course,
manifest in frightening and worrying ways. Now what
I'm going to do is prescribe you a course of—"

Richard Dixon shook his head fiercely. "No pills,
doctor. I'm sick to death of them. I'm telling you what
I see is real. He's there, every night. I can be there,
lying in bed, unable to sleep, when I hear him: footsteps, quiet footsteps, creeping up the stairs. I can see
the shadow under the door. And then the handle starts
to turn—"

Fordham sighed. "And then the door opens. And the

clown's there. Yes, yes, I've heard it all before."

"But it's true, I tell you."

"Mr. Dixon. I see at least a dozen patients a week who all share similar fantasies to yourself. With some it's giant spiders, with others it's paintings that talk. Each has their own bogeyman, their own personal fear, which, for some reason or other, their mind turns into some form of nightmare. But that's all it is. A form of nightmare. These things exist in the same way that ghosts and demons do. In other words, they exist only up here." He gently tapped his head. "Now, I really do recommend that you take the pills that I'm going to prescribe you. At the very least, they'll help you sleep better."

Dixon rose from the chair he had been sitting at. He glared across at Fordham. "I can tell that you don't believe me, doctor, that you think I'm just imagining all of this. Perhaps you ascribe it all to stress and over-work. But I can tell you, with one hundred percent certainty, that this thing does exist, and not just in my head. And what's more, I'm going to prove it." With that, he retrieved his coat and hat from the hat-stand and stormed out.

* * * * * * *

The next morning, the telephone on Fordham's desk began to ring. He reached out and picked it up. "Good morning, Doctor Fordham here. How can I help?"

"Doctor." The voice on the other end of the line sounded extremely agitated. "May I come round and see you immediately? It's Richard Dixon."

"Ah, Mr. Dixon. I'm afraid I'm busy most of this morning. I have several patient appointments. Why don't you get in touch with my secretary and we can see about—"

"I need to see you straight away, doctor. It's regarding what we were talking about yesterday. I think you'll find it very interesting."

"As I said, Mr. Dixon, I have a very busy morning ahead of me. Perhaps I can see you briefly this afternoon. Shall we say one o'clock? But it will have to be brief."

"Very well. I'll see you then."

The phone went down.

Fordham stared at it confusedly for a moment. There had been something in the other's voice which was beginning to set off alarm bells within him. He consulted his watch and realised he had twenty minutes before his next patient arrived, so there was time enough for him to briefly go over his notes regarding Dixon. Reaching into a drawer in his filing cabinet, he soon found the documentation pertaining to the man in question. He began to skim through what he had written.

Dixon was vice-president of a large pharmaceutical company based here in the city. By all accounts, he was a fairly wealthy man. Unmarried, he had thrown himself into his career, climbing quickly up the corporate ladder so that now, aged forty-one, he was hotly tipped to take over when the incumbent president stepped down. His childhood was unremarkable, with no signs of any childhood phobias short of a general and rather healthy fear of dogs. Both his parents were still alive and his relationship with them was of the highest sort. His favourite colour was blue and on all of the routine psychometric tests he had fallen well within the 'so-called' normal range. He enjoyed reading all manner of books and he was quite good at bowls. The topic of alcohol consumption had been raised and dismissed as a contributory factor. In short, apart from this profound delusional fear of a nightmarish clown—something that had only manifested recently—there was absolutely nothing in his history or genetic make-up to account for this brush with insanity.

* * * * * * *

At one o'clock precisely, the door to Fordham's office swung open and Dixon stepped inside. He was wearing a long grey raincoat that was sodden and a dark hat. In his hands, which Fordham noted were shaking quite badly, he clutched a brown envelope.

"Mr. Dixon. I hope you realise that my time is—"

"Doctor, I need you to take a look at this." Dixon opened the brown envelope and removed a copy of a rather tacky-looking paperback and put it down on the desk. He sat down.

Fordham stared confusedly at the garish cover, which showed a man dressed in a top hat and cape staring into a mirror. His reflection was that of a skeleton.

"*Supernatural Stories?* I can't say that I've ever—"

"No, not the book," said Dixon, shaking it by the spine so that a photograph slipped free from the confines of its pages. He picked it up. "Take a look, doctor. Take a good look and then tell me that I'm mad, that I'm imagining all this." He handed the photograph to the other.

Curious, Fordham stared hard at the rather grainy image. His eyes narrowed and then widened as he began to discern some of the details. It showed what he assumed was his patient's bedroom door, slightly ajar. It was hard to be clear, and did require some level of imagination on his own part, but was that the fingers of a gloved hand creeping around the door frame? He squinted again, tracing the blurry image with his index finger, trying to discern the shadowy shape. His heart lurched when he thought he could make out a cast shadow, a bulbous nose, strangely jagged hair. He swallowed a lump in his throat. No, he tried to tell himself, that was only his imagination, his self-projection. He cleared his head, and the clown-like shape and the hand had now assumed nothing more sinister than the dark shape and shadow of a hung-up coat.

"Do you see it? It's there, isn't it?"

Fordham considered the photograph a final time. Yes, he thought, it would be very easy for someone— more so someone of Dixon's current mental state— to observe things that weren't really there, to create phantasms out of everyday things. It was a well-known phenomenon; one had only to note the ability that many had to 'see' shapes in clouds or the way in which some people insisted that they saw faces in knots of wood. In many ways it was a desire within an individual to 'see' what they wanted to 'see'. And yet, he had to admit that he had almost fallen into the trap.

"Well, isn't it?"

"There's nothing there, Mr. Dixon. Just shadows. Once again your mind has played tricks on you."

"But I saw it. I—I heard it opening the door. Dreams and nightmares can't do that, doctor. That's its hand I photographed. And you can see its shadow."

"A rather conveniently blurry image, wouldn't you agree, Mr. Dixon? I mean, let's face it, this could be anything. Now the question I ask myself, is if this thing does exist, then why didn't you get a better picture? Something rather more conclusive?"

"I did, but it disappeared."

"Once again, rather convenient, don't you think? You see, I'm a pragmatic, rational man. I accept evidence when I see it. But, there's nothing here. It's like these photographs people claim to have taken of flying saucers. They're always out of focus, taken by complete amateurs with no idea of photography. Consequently, it's very easy to dismiss them as nothing more than natural phenomenon or deliberate hoaxes. But anyway, can you tell me why you chose to take this photograph?"

"I'd have thought that was rather obvious. I wanted to prove to you that this thing exists. I can't sleep at night any more. It's driving me insane. And if the only way that you will accept that it exists is to see a photograph of it—"

"Mr. Dixon. How many times must I tell you this thing does not exist. You're becoming fixated with it. Try to relax and forget all about it." Fordham was becoming exasperated. He was fast beginning to think that his patient was a lost cause. Without recourse to pills, he felt he had exhausted all of the standard means of support and assistance that he could offer.

"Please doctor, I'm begging you. You have to believe me." Dixon's words were now bordering on the pathetic. It was abundantly clear that this irrational phobia was scaring the life out of him, and that unless there was some means of conquering this fear, or of eradicating it completely, then he faced the prospect of going irrevocably insane. "I'm finding that I'm unable to work any more. I can't sleep at night for fear that it will—"

Fordham straightened in his seat and interlocked his long fingers. "Will what? Just what is it you fear this imaginary thing will do?"

"Kill me, strangle me in my sleep—or scare me to death maybe. I've no doubt its intentions are harmful."

"But clowns are benign things, comical things, things of ridicule. We take our children to see them at the circus. How can they be frightening?" Fordham swallowed a lump in his throat. He could imagine how frightening the uncanny appearance of a bizarrely-outfitted thing, its face done up in garish make-up, its hair wild and unruly, might be when seen in the dead of night.

"It just is. It's terrible. A horror." In a surprising movement, Dixon got down on his knees and began to beg. His whole body was trembling and he clasped his hands together. "Please, doctor, help me. It's ruining my life. You must help me."

Worriedly, Fordham rubbed his chin. In his mind he was trying to work out just how exactly he could help. His options seemed limited. The other had point-blankly refused to consider any form of medication. All his forms of therapy had likewise proved unsuccessful. He felt helpless, resigned almost and that in itself troubled his conscience. It was not like him to desert a patient in their time of need. He gulped. "I'm afraid there's little more that I can do, Mr. Dixon." He shook his head gravely. "Unless you're prepared to take the medication on offer—"

Dixon got to his feet. "So that's it. You admit there is nothing that can be done. Very well, I hope you can sleep easily at night, because I know I can't." He got to his feet and stormed out of the office once more.

* * * * * * *

It was Dixon's screams that prompted the neighbours to call for the police. They smashed their way into his house and found the unfortunate curled up on his bed, dressed only in his pyjamas, staring fixedly at the bedroom door. The look on his face was one of sheer horror, and they were able to only get a few coherent words from him. In the end, as they escorted him downstairs into his living room, some of the words began to make more sense. Something about a clown. Gradually, he began to become more normal, taking some of the coffee that was offered to him. In the end, he managed to divulge the phone number of his treating clinician and an hour or so later Fordham, slightly weary-looking himself, turned up at the house. He was greeted by one of the policemen.

"Sorry to be getting you out at this time of night, doctor, but it seems as though our friend here's in desperate need of psychiatric evaluation and assistance." The policeman gestured to Dixon who now sat at his kitchen table, eyes wide and bloodshot, his entire body shaking. Slowly, he began to spoon mouthfuls of cereal into his quivering mouth.

"Has he said anything?" inquired Fordham.

"Not much that made any sense, if that's what you're saying. He did mutter something about a clown or something. It was rather hard to make out just what he was talking about. It was his screams that roused the neighbours. I'm no expert, but I'd say he's had a dreadful nightmare. Strange thing is, though, we found this on the landing just outside his door."

Fordham's heart lurched somewhat as the policeman delved into his pocket and removed a small black pompom.

* * * * * * *

Fordham sat wiggling the tip of his pen between his teeth—opposite him, looking haggard, unshaven, and withdrawn was Dixon. The doctor had stayed sitting up with his patient for most of the night, before, at the other's insistence driving him to his surgery where he had bunked down in the one and only medical ward.

It was now morning and Fordham could not help but feel that he was letting himself be dragged into something he would rather not get involved with. Nevertheless, the man was his patient, and if there remained any possibility of prolonging or indeed saving his sanity, it was up to him to try and do it. The discovery of the pompom had him slightly confused, and he had deliberated over it for most of the morning. Now he thought he had the explanation—the other had placed it there to be found. It seemed obvious the more he considered it. The other possible alternative that he had contemplated was that his patient had unknowingly put it there, although that implied a deeper form of psychosis, for it meant that Dixon was playing into the hands of his own delusion; actively promoting his own insanity, creating his own nightmare and giving it a physicality. He had read about such cases in some of his neuropsychological journals.

"I know you don't believe me, but I saw it."

"Did you have your camera, Mr. Dixon? Did you get any more photographs?"''

"No. Not this time."

"And why was that?"

"I was too frightened. It was its laugh, you see."

"Laugh?" Fordham jotted something down in his notebook.

"Terrible laughter. Horrible. I could hear it as it came

up the stairs, growing louder as it neared my bedroom door."

"I see. And was that the first time you've heard this laughter?"

"Yes. I think so. It's all rather confusing." Dixon looked straight at the doctor, a soul-weary, exhausted look on his face. "You think I'm cracking up, don't you doctor? It'll be the white-coated men with the butterfly nets for me, won't it? I bet even now you're reserving me a room with padded wallpaper at the Chester-Brooke Mental Asylum."

"That's a rather paranoid thought, don't you think Mr. Dixon?"

"But true nonetheless, yes? You're going to get me, what's the word—*committed*—that's right isn't it? Locked up out of harm's way with all of the other nutters."

"I've no intention of doing that."

"No?"

"No. Absolutely not."

"Then you believe me? About the clown?"

"Did I say that?" Fordham threw the other a questioning glance. "Mr. Dixon, I don't know how many times I have to repeat myself— *There is no clown.*" His words were slow and enunciated. "However, having said that, there's clearly something within your psychology which may be predisposed to—"

The phone on the desk began to ring.

"If you'll excuse me a moment." Fordham picked it up. "Doctor Fordham here. I'm with a patient at the moment, so if you will excuse——"

He paused, a confused look on his face.

Dixon's heart jumped. "It's him, isn't it? The clown?"

"Sorry, it's a bit of a bad line. Could you repeat?" Fordham's face strained somewhat as he tried to listen. "*Mr. Dixon?* Yes, he's here with me at the moment. Who is this and how did you get this number?" After a pause: "Ah, I see. Well yes, Mr. Dixon is receiving some help at the moment, but I'm not at liberty to talk about either his diagnosis or his treatment. Yes, I see your predicament Mr. Carlyle."

Recognition struck Dixon. The doctor was speaking to the president of his firm.

"No, I can't be more precise. Yes, his condition could be described as chronic, but with proper care and treatment——" A pause, as Fordham listened to what the other was saying. "No, I don't think there will be any long-lasting effects. Now if you don't mind." Once more a long, drawn-out pause. There was a look of growing impatience on the doctor's face. "Well, I can assure you, Mr. Carlyle, I don't see that as an option, certainly not at the moment. Yes I do have the necessary authorisation, but I see no need. Now if you don't mind, I really do have to get back to my patient. Good day." He put the phone down.

Dixon looked questioningly across the table.

"As you have no doubt realised, that was the president of your firm. I must say I don't think I'd like to have him as my superior."

"He can be a bit awkward at times. But basically

I'd say he's a good man, a powerful man with lots of contacts. It's clear he's quite concerned about me."

Yes, thought Fordham. *Very concerned.* And then, a highly-suspicious thought went through his mind. Dixon worked for a leading pharmaceutical company—was it just possible that mind-altering, nightmare-inducing drugs were on its list of products? It was a possibility he had to concede—and therefore it was equally possible that Dixon had come into contact with them. It was also conceivable that he was being used as a human guinea pig. Desperately, Fordham tried to shrug that thought away—to lock it in some dark recess. Surely no responsible company would operate in such a callous and illegal manner?

Looking at Dixon, Fordham could see that one thing was clear: he feared for the man's sanity if he had to endure another night of mental torture. He was now at the most dangerous and vulnerable of stages, and he knew that one more shock was quite likely to tip him over the edge, to drive him into that black abyss of screaming madness from which few, if any, ever returned.

* * * * * *

After telling Dixon where he was going and leaving him in the care of one of his junior doctors, Fordham got in his car and drove out to the massive pharma-ceutical factory, which lay on the outskirts of the city. He seldom came out this way, although he was fairly familiar with the route, and the directions to it were well signposted. It was a clear morning, the sky possessing that freshly rain-washed quality that enabled him to make out the multiple chimneys and outlying structures clearly. The place was enormous, a veritable chemical processing site dedicated to the manufacturing of countless pharmaceutical products.

Inwardly, he was wondering just why he had got himself involved in all of this. It surely went far above and beyond the normal doctor-patient relationship. And yet, constantly niggling at the back of his mind, there was that growing suspicion that there was something not quite right going on here. He doubted whether it warranted any kind of official investigation, such as getting the police involved, but even so, there was definitely something which he was finding hard to swallow, like a fishbone stuck at the back of his throat, unable to be shifted. Just what it was, he intended to find out. Ever since Dixon had first walked into his clinic, citing his current preoccupation, he had always had some level of suspicion that there was something deeper going on than just one man's delusions.

There was a detectable chemical smell in the air that he readily identified as ethyl acetate. At the main entrance checkpoint he flashed his doctor's identification card and was allowed free entry, making some excuse or other about how he was here to attend a meeting on the findings of a new drug trial.

Parking his car in the staff car park, he got out of his vehicle and walked towards the grand-looking reception and slightly futuristic administration building. A glass elevator on the outside went up many floors to the very roof, from which numerous flags and emblems with the company logo were prominently displayed. Everything gleamed richly in the brilliant sunlight, lending the place an innovative, state of the art look. It was abundantly clear that several millions of pounds had been spent on this building alone.

Walking through the shining glass doors, Fordham entered the main lobby, an equally extravagant affair. Faint, pleasing to the ear classical music hummed gently. He went straight up to the reception desk and the attractive female receptionist behind it.

"Good morning. My name is Doctor Fordham. I'm a good friend of Richard Dixon, your vice-president. I was wondering if I could have a word with Mr. Carlyle?"

"I'm afraid Mr. Carlyle is a very busy man, sir. Unless you have an appointment, I seriously doubt whether he'll be able to see you." Her manner was polite and courteous, but there was a certain sternness to her voice.

"I do have an appointment," Fordham lied. "Well, in a manner of speaking. You see I'm here on behalf of Mr. Dixon, who is currently indisposed."

"I'm very sorry, sir, but as I said, Mr. Carlyle is a very busy man, and he's given explicit orders not to be disturbed. Now, if there's any thing else I can do for you?"

"Would you put a call through to him? I'm sure that once he understood why I'm here, he'd—"

"I'm sorry sir, but he was very adamant that he should not be disturbed."

The secretary's intransigence was beginning to grate on the doctor's nerves. He was just about to come up with some other plan of attack, when opportunity came knocking as a voice behind him said:

"Is there any way in which I can assist you?" The voice was refined and cultured.

Fordham turned to see a smartly-dressed young man in a dark suit. In one hand he held a thick dossier. In the other he clutched a blue hard hat.

"Mr. Carlyle, sir," started the secretary, "this gentleman here requests to see your father."

"Is that so? And just what may I ask is the purpose of your visit?"

"It's concerning Mr. Dixon. I'm his treating clinician, Doctor Fordham." For the briefest of moments Fordham could have sworn he saw something sinister glint within the other's eyes. Under normal circumstances he would have offered his hand to shake, but there was something about the other that he didn't like although he couldn't quite place why, so he kept his hand in his pocket.

"Ah, poor Richard. He's keeping well, I hope. My father told me he's been away from work for a week or so. Nothing serious, I trust?"

"He's getting better, if that's what you mean."

"Glad to hear it, he's such an—essential part of our team."

"I'll be sure to pass on your comments." Fordham

decided to change tack. "It's quite an impressive set-up you have here. Can you tell me just what it is you do?" he asked.

"We produce a wide range of pharmaceutical products, much of which are sent abroad. We're also diversifying into the field of cosmetics, pesticides, and synthetic-food development. It's a very interesting time for the company as our markets are expanding. My father has just negotiated a very lucrative and far-reaching contract with the United States agricultural sector. In addition, we also provide employment for the local community, as this is the single largest employer in the area. Additionally, unlike some of our rivals, we believe in a solid ecological philosophy, recycling much of our own waste."

Fordham came straight out with it. "What about hallucinogens?"

"No, nothing like that. Some would say the world is a mad enough place without us contributing to it by manufacturing anything that alters the mind. We're a highly ethical company which takes its responsibilities strongly."

"I'm glad to hear that. Now I fully understand that your time and mine is precious, so is there any chance of—"

"Meeting my father? I'm afraid not. You see he's actually not here at the moment. He's at home. It's where he prefers to do much of his business. He did say that he would be in some time tomorrow though. I'll see to it that you get a chance to meet him. In the meantime, I'm sure you'll appreciate that I've got quite a lot to do. There's a big plant inspection that I need to oversee." He put on his safety helmet. "Anyway, it's been nice meeting you and please do pass on my kindest regards to Richard and my wishes for a speedy recovery." He headed off for the main entrance.

With something of a sense of disappointment, Fordham watched him go. He checked his watch. There was little point in him staying here. He would head back, perhaps getting a light lunch somewhere and then see how his patient was doing. The thought that perhaps he himself was beginning to read too much into what was transpiring struck him with a fierce suddenness. Dixon's problems were bad enough without him having to theorise malicious conspiracy theories. Perhaps it *was* just a case of delusional thought processes that were plaguing the other. Yet, there remained that small kernel of inner doubt within him, some small element of suspicion that there was something darker behind all of this, some malign purpose. This view had been reinforced by his telephone conversation with the elder Carlyle—for it had seemed that the president of the firm had been in some kind of hurry to get Dixon committed. Why? Well, that remained the issue. He had once read a story in which a man had gone to quite elaborate lengths, such as wiring up the house in such a manner as to simulate a ghostly haunting, to drive his wife insane so that he could profit financially. Could it be conceivable that something similar was happening here? Could it be that Carlyle and his son were involved in some diabolical plan to enforce madness on Dixon, and if so, was this being done with the involvement of drugs? A simple blood test would confirm this one way or another. But, of course, obtaining the results would take time. And time, right now, was something Fordham did not think was on their side, for it was his belief that with one more appearance of the imaginary clown, Dixon would be lost forever. That being the case, it gave him till nightfall.

* * * * * * *

It had just gone three o'clock in the afternoon when Fordham stepped into his surgery. He was quite pleased to see that Dixon was looking a bit better. But that was now, how would he be when the shadows lengthened and the clown came tiptoeing its way through his house, its hideous-sounding, gurgling laughter echoing off the walls?

"He'll come again tonight, won't he? The clown, I mean."

"I very much doubt that, Mr. Dixon." With a brief thanks, Fordham dismissed his junior doctor. "You're looking much better than you did earlier in the day. I tried to get to see Mr. Carlyle, but unfortunately he was not available. I did see his son briefly, who told me to pass on his best wishes for a speedy recovery."

"That would be William. A conniving, scheming youngster. It's common knowledge that he's been after my position for quite some time now."

Fordham raised an eyebrow. "Is that so? I must say

he struck me too as a rather arrogant and self-important young man. Certainly ambitious. No doubt he intends to step into his old man's shoes at some time in the near future."

"Wouldn't surprise me in the slightest."

"Anyway, Mr. Dixon, the situation that now faces us is this: sometime this evening you will have to go home, since you can't stay here indefinitely. And as a one-off I am prepared to stay over at your place to help you get through the night. One night at a time, Mr. Dixon. That's the way to proceed. If you can get through this night, you can get through all nights. Remember what I have told you and keep repeating it to yourself. Let this become your mantra: *There is no clown. There is no clown.* Just keep saying it over and over to yourself. Now if you'll make your way to my car, I'll just get some things and I'll join you shortly."

* * * * * * *

The early evening traffic was building up and the pleasantness of the day had now been replaced with heavy rain showers, which impeded their progress towards Dixon's suburban house. Fordham had to ask his passenger twice for directions. Eventually, however, they pulled into the driveway, the tyres crunching on the loose gravel.

Removing a large overnight bag from the boot, Fordham followed his patient up to the big house. It was raining heavily now and both men were thankful for their raincoats. Thunder rumbled in the distance.

The house seemed to have a dark and foreboding appearance.

"I'm so scared," Dixon shivered, staring up at his house. "I don't think I can go back in there. He's close, I'm sure of it."

"Calm down." Fordham looked up at the rambling house with those many windows that seemed to look down at them like dark eyes. However, it was what possibly lay beyond the windows, in the darkened rooms, that sent a small tremor of fear through him. He gulped nervously, and tried to get a firm hold of himself. What good would it do his patient if he were to show signs of worry? "Remember your mantra. *There is no clown.*"

"There is no clown." Dixon mumbled the phrase unconvincingly.

"Come on, let's get inside."

The front door had been only half-heartedly repaired after the police had broken it down the previous night and a large padlock now secured it.

"It doesn't matter. I lost my front door key a while ago," said Dixon. "We'll be able to go in the back door." He removed a key from his pocket.

They went around to the side of the house and entered the property using the back door. The kitchen they went into was just as Fordham remembered it.

Dixon flicked a light switch and instant brightness chased away the darkness. His eyes were wild and roving, darting all around. It was clear to the doctor that his patient was taking in everything with the eyes of someone who was half-expecting some laughing, giggling, bizarre figure to leap out from the opposite doorway. In reality, Dixon's fractured mind was thinking along even more surreal channels—that the clown would emerge from the kitchen sink or else from a food cupboard, its body horribly concertinaed like a compressed contortionist.

There was nothing of the sort, of course. It was just a kitchen—plain and nondescript; a bachelor's kitchen.

Fordham shut the back door. "Why don't I see about making us something to eat? I warn you, my culinary skills aren't up to much, but I can at least heat up a tin of soup."

Dixon merely nodded. With wooden, fear-filled steps he slowly crossed the kitchen to the short passage that joined the hall. He switched on all the lights he came to, every single one.

Soon all the lights on the ground floor were on.

Dixon hesitated when he came to the foot of the stairs. Above him, everything was in shadow, dark and menacing. For a moment, he thought he saw something move within the clinging darkness, and he felt a sudden riot of fear and horror grip his brain. Was this clown a ghost of some description? This was a new thought and one that he had never considered before. Could it be that a man who had been a clown had died here—and his tortured spirit now remained? It was possible. Hell—anything was possible, he told himself. The doctor's sudden shout startled him and made him jump.

"Soup's ready. Minestrone. If it tastes as good as it smells we're in for a treat."

The rather basic meal was a meal of silences, for it was clear that Dixon was extremely troubled and he said nothing, eating mechanically. Once they had finished, the doctor tidied the bowls and cutlery away.

They then spent several hours playing cards, somewhat uneasy in each other's company and at the prospect of what the night might bring. It was really just a question of whiling away the hours until retiring for the night.

Outside, the storm grew in ferocity.

"If you'll come upstairs with me, I'll show you to the spare room. I'm too scared to go up on my own."

"After you then." Fordham picked up his overnight bag and followed the other out into the hall.

Dixon hesitated once more at the foot of the stairs. Marshalling his courage and knowing that he was accompanied, he began the climb.

"Remember, keep telling yourself, 'there is no clown'."

Repeating these words to himself, they gradually made it to the landing where Dixon took a deep sigh of relief. He felt somewhat bolstered by this small achievement. One fear had been overcome, now it was just a question of whether or not he could make it through the night.

As though Fordham had read his thoughts, he said: "Are you sure I can't give you something to help you sleep easier? From the look of you, what you could be doing with more than anything is a good night's sleep."

Dixon shook his head. "No thanks." He pointed to a door at the end of the short corridor. "That's your room."

"Well, I guess all I can say is sleep well. Goodnight." Fordham went to his room and settled down for the night.

* * * * * * *

Fordham came awake swiftly and sharply, that part of his mind which had learned never to fully sleep dragging him back to consciousness at the faintest flicker of sound. For a long moment, he lay there on the small bed, searching around in the darkness of the room with eyes and ears, straining to pick out the sound that had woken him, to identify it and pinpoint its location. Moonlight shone in through the double set of windows providing reasonable illumination.

Then it came again; the faint sound of someone—or something—moving in the small en-suite bathroom. The sounds were faint, but he was sure it was not his imagination. Sliding out of bed, he dressed quietly so as not to disturb whatever was making the noise. Then, stealthily he made his way towards the door. It was as he was nearing it that he saw the handle beginning to turn.

His heart jittered. There was someone in there!

Slowly, the door began to open.

Gulping in fear, Fordham watched in utter bewilderment as the opening widened, revealing the dark space beyond. Within the darkness, he thought he saw something, but squinting his eyes and peering harder, trying to throw his sight into the shadows, he was now not so certain. Yet the door had opened—how had that happened? Mustering his courage, he crept forward, now crossing the threshold into the small room. Blindly, he reached out with his left hand for a light switch, certain that at any moment something dark and grasping would take a hold of him and pull him inside, drag him away into some screaming nightmare.

He flicked the switch.

The clown was there! Its face was chalk-white, its eyes inverted crosses of blackness. A bulbous red nose and a mouth, blackened with lipstick, stared crazily at him. His mind darkened.

* * * * * * *

Two days later, Fordham drove his car up the long, tree-lined avenue that led to the Chester-Brooke Mental Asylum. In his rear view mirror he could see the security gate now dwindling from sight, the gate guard having returned to his office. For the time being everything outside felt calm, eerily tranquil, and yet his own mind was now in something of a turmoil. He felt certain that something had happened to him back in Dixon's house, something bizarre and inexplicable, something that defied all reason and explanation. But what exactly it was he couldn't quite place. Had he seen something? His memory of that time was warped and scrambled, and despite his best efforts to try and remember, he was not quite sure.

What he was sure about, though, was that Dixon was now, without any doubt, incurably mad. That night at his patient's house had been one of sheer horror. One in which he, despite his medical training, had been unable to fully come to terms with. He had remembered Dixon screaming, constantly screaming as a summoned ambulance crew had dragged him down the stairs and carried him out. He had been raving, his eyes wide and full of madness.

And now he was here. And in all likelihood this would now be his permanent address.

Parking his car in the car park, Fordham got out and walked up to the imposing, Victorian-built asylum. There was a certain finality in the grim architecture that he looked at, giving the building a depressing and foreboding appearance. For many, this was as far as they ever got. It was undoubtedly like a prison for many, he thought.

A nurse could been seen pushing an old man who was shaking and talking to himself in a wheelchair around the garden.

Nearing the main entrance, Fordham was somewhat surprised to see William, the younger Carlyle, leaning against the porch, smoking a cigarette. Suppressing a small sense of dislike, he walked towards the man.

"We meet again," he said.

William removed the cigarette from his mouth. "Yes, hello." He took another drag. "A sad business this, regarding Richard. I wasn't aware that things had got quite so bad."

"A sad business indeed. At least in here he'll hopefully be free from his torment."

"Let's hope so. By the way, my father's inside, if you wanted to have a word. We came out here to meet with the medical staff and to see if there was any way in which we could be of assistance. It seemed the least we could do. They wouldn't allow us to see Richard, which is quite understandable under the circumstances, I suppose."

Fordham half-smiled. Once again, he had that slightly unnerving feeling about the younger Carlyle, something which he couldn't put his finger on. "I'll go in and see your father, then." Pushing open the main entrance door, he found himself in the large reception area. A late middle-aged, well-dressed man wearing a pair of old-fashioned, circular spectacles strode purposefully towards him.

"What about you? You look like a doctor. Are you going to tell me what's going on here?"

Fordham was somewhat taken aback by the angry tone in the other's voice. "Excuse me?"

"Me and my son have had nothing but the runaround since we got here. We've come here to find out how a friend of ours and a work colleague—"

"Mr. Dixon?" Fordham extended his hand and the other shook it. "Yes, I'm your work colleague's psychiatrist. I take it, therefore, that you are Mr. Carlyle. I'm pleased to meet you. Unfortunately, however it's not very good news regarding Richard. Shall we go into

one of the offices where we can talk more freely?"

The two of them headed off towards one of the side rooms. Once inside, Fordham closed the door and gestured to Carlyle to take a seat. He then sat down opposite him. "Well, I'm sure you know that unfortunately Mr. Dixon has been admitted here. I know in our previous phone conversation I told you that I did not think it necessary to have him transferred here, but unfortunately his condition has since deteriorated. I was with him the night that it was deemed necessary to bring him here, both for his own and for the safety of others. Although I don't think he poses any real danger, he's obviously in quite a delusional state of mind such that anything is possible. Hence, I see this as a purely precautionary measure."

"And how long will he be in here? Indefinitely?"

"That's hard to say. It all depends on whether he can make any steps to recovery. But such a recovery will take time, and we're not talking days or weeks, but rather, months, perhaps years."

"Can you arrange for me to see him? Who knows, I might be able to talk sense into him where you've been unable. Surely, it's worth a try."

Fordham shook his head. "I'm afraid—"

"Please. Richard's always been a good company man and I owe him a lot. The firm owes him a lot."

"Alright. I'll see what I can do." Fordham rose from his chair and left the office, leaving Carlyle alone for over ten minutes. He stepped back inside. "Could you come this way?" he announced.

Deeper into the asylum they went, the long passages eerily quiet and empty. There were few medical staff around.

"It's a wonder you can work in a place like this," commented Carlyle. "The place give me the chills."

"I don't normally work here. My main clinic is in the city." Fordham opened a door and held it open for the other. "If you'll just wait a few minutes in here, I'll go and get Mr. Dixon. Now that I've completed the necessary clearance documentation, it shouldn't be long. It's just a case of getting him from his—" He was on the verge of saying "cell," but then quickly corrected himself; "Room," he finished with a smile.

After an uncomfortable ten minutes during which the apprehension within Carlyle began to burn like mild acid within his gut, the door opened and Richard walked in. This was not the foaming at the mouth lunatic, manhandled by two burly, white-coated orderlies, he had half-expected, but rather a broken, grey-faced shell of a man who was clearly so detached from reality that he might as well have been on another planet. This was no longer a man Carlyle recognised.

In clothes that no longer fitted him, Dixon looked gravely ill, almost death-like. His skin was greyish, sallow, and wrinkled, his eyes sunken and vacant, devoid of life. His hair was wild, and looked like it had never been introduced to a comb before. There was an unpleasant smell coming from him. A man of forty-one now looked like a sick man in his eighties. He was mindless, nothing more than a zombie.

It was the shock more than anything else that struck Carlyle. For now, having seen his one-time work colleague with his own eyes, and having seen the degrading transformation, he now knew that there was no real hope for his friend. Words failed him, and all he could do was shake his head in dismay and look at Fordham, half-words trying to mouth themselves into something coherent.

Fordham simply nodded, understandingly, and guided Dixon away again.

* * * * * * *

"I'm really so grateful to you doctor." With trembling hands, William Carlyle poured himself another glass of whisky. He had now consumed almost three-quarters of the bottle. He looked dishevelled and red-eyed, unshaven and slovenly. "Nobody else believes me. But it's real, I tell you. You know what happened to Dixon. You were there."

Fordham studied the other with deeply concerned eyes. He put down his overnight bag. "I don't believe in this clown, but I do believe in your distress." He eyed the whisky bottle. "I think you should stop drinking now and I'll help you upstairs to your bedroom."

"No! I'm not going to sleep. Never. That's when he comes."

"Alright, we'll talk for a while longer." Sitting in an armchair, Fordham's old theory returned to his mind. Both Dixon and Carlyle had worked at the same pharmaceutical company; therefore, he thought, it was not implausible that they were both suffering from some chemical effect—an effect which had claimed Dixon's sanity less than a month ago, and was now quickly eroding Carlyle's. "Are you sure you can think of nothing at the factory, nothing dangerous that you might have come into contact with?"

Carlyle groaned. "There's nothing, I tell you." He drank from his glass, his eyes becoming more glazed, then slumped to one side, his head in his hands.

Fordham sighed and carefully removed the empty glass from the young man's hand. He was past protesting, and so the doctor hefted the other's feet onto the sofa and looked around for a rug to cover Carlyle with. By the time he had found one, his charge was fast asleep. Best thing for him, Fordham thought.

He decided to find the guest room for himself, and set off down a corridor in the modern, expensively furnished house. As he walked past one of the many mirrors he caught sight of something at the edge of his vision, a flash of colour. Turning quickly he scanned the corridor, but there was nothing there. He continued on, but in the next mirror, once again there was something. As he tried to scrutinise it, it vanished. Shaking now, he neared the third and final mirror on the wall.

His eyes widened in terror as he approached, mesmerised. The horror was terribly familiar inside his brain, even as the slight smile began to grow on his face. Then he was transforming, changing once more, for the reflection was he and he was it. The Harlequin of Fear, Demon Prince of Madness, shed the mortal vestige of his disguise and the thing that was Doctor Fordham—that oblivious, pathetic alter ego—sloughed away, melting like thawing ice. The wild hair, bulbous nose, cruel black painted lips replaced the friendly visage, and the doctor's clothes became the clown's garish, black-and-white-chequered, collar-frilled costume.

Looking with approval at its horrific, true self, the Harlequin of Fear chuckled before turning and stalking back to the sleeping form of William Carlyle.

THE UNEARTHED

There was a very good reason why the dead remained buried.

Seated in the wide passenger seat of the mud-spattered van, Mike Salisbury filled in some of the details of the archaeological report pertaining to the discovery that he and his team members had made just over an hour ago. On the dashboard in front of him rested a flask and a cup of steaming coffee. He reached out for the cup and took a drink, wincing somewhat as the hot liquid burnt his tongue.

He was getting mild eyestrain from doing the paperwork, so he turned to look out of the window at the heavy drizzle as it came down in grey sheets on the expanse of bleak moorland. In the distance, he could see his two associates in their blue waterproofs, their forms barely visible through the rain, some three hundred yards away. He was about to return to the form he was in the process of completing when he heard their agitated shouts. Quickly, he zipped up his waterproof, pulled the hood up, then clambered out of the vehicle.

"What is it?" he shouted, squelching through the

ankle-deep mud, excitement fuelling his every step. About him, the land was wide and open—a desolate, boggy, fog-filled heath with few trees to offer shelter from the wind and the rain. Over to his right, barely discernible, were the tenebrous outlines of some high tors.

"We've got another!" one of the men called back.

Shaking off the cold and wet, Salisbury trudged forward. A few minutes later, he saw his two friends, their faces smeared with mud. Robert Matthews stood in a waist-deep, waterlogged trench, his visible upper half reminding Salisbury somewhat of the bog body they had already pulled from the dank earth. James Shaw, the third and youngest and least experienced archaeologist, stood to one side, resting nonchalantly on a spade.

"What do you make of this?" asked Matthews, pointing.

Salisbury knelt at the edge of the excavation, his eyes drawn to the discoloured, bag-shaped protuberance that the other indicated. Delicately, he reached down, touching the spongy, long-dead flesh.

"I've never known anything like it," said Matthews. "To find one bog body is pretty amazing, but two? And so close together."

"I guess I'll have to go and get the sheet of tarpaulin again, won't I?" said Shaw.

"If you'd be so good," replied Salisbury. "We're also going to need some of those small plastic bags so that we can get some more samples from the surrounding soil. We need to confirm that this bog body is from the same context as the first one. Just by looking at the stratigraphy of the trench, I'd guess that it is. However, we could do with having proof of this."

"How many bags will you be needing?" asked Shaw.

"A dozen should be fine." Salisbury removed the trowel from where it hung at his belt and lowered himself carefully into the damp trench, watching as the dispatched Shaw vanished into the rain. "All right," he said to Matthews, "let's see what we have here."

With the use of their trowels the two archaeologists began to clear clods of thick, sticky earth from around the body. Digging into the side of the trench, they began to expose more and more of the preserved corpse.

With the help of his colleague, Salisbury supported the gruesome find. Then, like mud-covered midwives, they carefully extricated it from the dank earth in which it had been encased for centuries.

"Good God!" exclaimed Matthews. "He's almost complete!"

"Well, you're right about one thing. He is a he," laughed Salisbury, noting the naturally pickled genitals. "Come on, let's get him onto the surface. This rain'll keep him moist enough till Shaw gets back with the tarpaulin and we can get him under cover."

Gingerly, the two men lifted the dirty, damp human remains out of the trench. Resting the body on the ground, they then began a cursory examination.

One arm hung limply, terminating in a fingerless lump, whilst the other was missing completely, undoubtedly sheared off by some passing peat-cutter. The age-old cadaver's head resembled little more than a pulped mass, within which the crooked line of a split mouth and one puffy, closed eye were still visible. The torso itself was relatively well preserved; traces of ribs and a clavicle poking out from under the wet, taut skin. One leg extended down to just above the right knee. The other leg was missing.

The main similarity with the first bog body that now lay in the back of the van, however, was the terribly severed throat.

Salisbury gulped deeply. "Just look at that! It's a wonder that his head wasn't severed completely."

"You realise this is going to be huge? Our careers are going to be assured after this."

Salisbury nodded and presented the other with a gleeful grin. Suddenly, an irregularity in the wall of the trench attracted his attention. Curious, he walked to one end of it, then knelt down, his trained eyes scanning the damp, black earth. Delicately, he probed his trowel into the surface before dislodging a clod of peaty deposit.

With a squelch, a lump of earth slid free, revealing a dark brown, putty-like face!

"Oh my God!" exclaimed Salisbury, falling back and landing on his backside.

"What?" shouted Matthews.

"*There's another!* This is absolutely unreal! Three in the same trench!" Salisbury gawped down at the ghastly face half-emerging from the layers of wet earth, the rain striking it for the first time in nigh on two thousand years, washing away some of the mud.

Matthews stared. Then, stepping over the bog body they had already dug out, he crouched down in the trench alongside Salisbury and together both men freed their third find. This one also showed signs of excessive violence. All the limbs were gone, the remains consisting of most of the head and half an upper torso.

Ten minutes passed as they studied the two bog bodies.

"Where the hell's Shaw?" asked Salisbury, impatiently. He and Matthews were now standing in the soaking rain over two unique archaeological finds. "We need to get the sheet of tarpaulin so that we can get these two under cover and back inside the van."

"My guess is that he's probably having a cup of coffee," answered Matthews. "Do you want me to go back and get him?"

"Give him another ten minutes."

Ten minutes came and went.

Both men tried to make conversation during that time, but the thrill of their discovery had now been replaced with concern over their missing associate. A further quarter of an hour passed and now Salisbury was becoming increasingly worried, trying to tell himself that Shaw was purposefully sitting in the van, sipping coffee and reading the newspaper they had picked up that morning from the nearest village post office, some fifteen miles away.

Eventually, Salisbury said: "I'll go get him," his

words startling Matthews.

"No, it's all right. I'll go," replied Matthews. For some reason he did not want to be left alone with the muddy human remains. For the past few minutes his mind had been working overtime, trying to keep in check the surreal thoughts of the two slimy things stirring to life and attacking him.

"Fair enough," said Salisbury, now sat on his haunches in the heavy drizzle. Thoroughly soaked, he silently cursed those of his associates who opted to work in sunnier climes. For a moment, he even began to feel the tug of a normal office job, a usual pull that came to him whenever his work brought him out to such godforsaken locations. He pushed back his sleeve and checked his watch. It was then that he heard Matthews call out Shaw's name. Twice, three times came the shout.

There was no reply!

Salisbury cursed under his breath. He sat there, for what seemed an eternity, feeling a numbing horror wash over him like the wildness of an incredible storm just past. His fingers twitched painfully at his side and terror threatened to overwhelm him utterly. There was a sudden panic in his heart and a dreadful feeling that something was very wrong indeed.

"I can't find Shaw! There's no sign of him!" shouted Matthews, making his way back through the gathering mist.

After a few minutes, Salisbury saw the form of Matthews emerging from the wet greyness. As he got nearer, he could see the worry on the other's face.

"He's not there," said Matthews, shaking his head confusedly. "He's nowhere to be seen."

"*What?* Where on earth can he be then?" Salisbury stared in utter bewilderment at his colleague. This was bordering on the insane. His eyes narrowed as he tried to fully comprehend what the other was telling him. *How was it possible that he could have just vanished?* There was a sensation of dull sickness in the pit of his stomach that persistently refused to go away and his brain felt curiously on fire. There was a strange tingling running along his limbs, as if a million tiny needles were probing beneath his skin.

"He can't have gone far."

Salisbury struggled to find his voice. "What about the stuff in the van? Is that still there, the tarpaulin and the bog body?"

"Yes, that's all in there all right." Matthews stared about him perplexedly, clearly distraught as to the younger man's disappearance. "I—I just can't under-stand this at all. It's as though he just—"

"*What?*" interrupted Salisbury. "Vanished into thin air?" He cursed savagely. "We'll be needing to get the local rescue teams out. This is just what we need right now. Where on earth could he have gone? It's not as though there's anything even remotely approaching civilisation within a ten-, maybe fifteen-mile radius of here." Dark tendrils of fear and worry reached out for his brain, threatening to suffocate all form of coherent thought. With a great mental effort, he forced them away. But even in their dismissal, there remained a small germ of distress that, in time, would threaten to overwhelm him, to engulf him like a terrible vine.

"What about mine shafts?" suggested Matthews, a tinge of worry now in his voice.

"There's nothing according to the maps."

"Do you think he might have headed for the village?"

Salisbury shook his head. "I can't see why. It's miles away. And why would he walk it?"

"He doesn't drive." Matthews reached into his pocket for the keys to the van. He wiggled them. "Besides, this is the only set."

"Yes, but that does not explain *why* he would go," argued, Salisbury. "And why'd he not tell us he was going? It just doesn't make any sense." Nothing about this made any sense to his mind. What had happened, and indeed was happening, was bordering on the inexplicable. It made no rhyme nor reason. One minute his colleague had been there, the next he had just disappeared. He wracked his brain for any kind of logical explanation and could find none. The harder he tried, the more troublesome the current situation became. His mind was now swirling with dark possibilities that he tried to rein in and keep in check.

"Well, what do we do now?" There was a look of deep concern on Matthews' face.

"God knows. Perhaps the best idea would be to try and see if you can somehow get the van up here so that we can get these two inside." Salisbury pointed at the two bog bodies. "Then we'll scout about for a bit, to see if we can find him. If we can't, we'll have to drive back to the village and see about getting the police out here. I imagine there'll be some kind of local rescue team or other."

"It'll be dark before anything like that can be arranged. Anyway, I'll see about getting the van up here." Matthews turned his back on the other and trudged off in the direction of the parked vehicle.

Troubled and angry, Salisbury sat down on the edge of the trench and watched as Matthews was once more enveloped in the mist. Inside, he could feel the nascent trembling of apprehension spread through his body as a sickly knot began to swell in his stomach. A feeling that something was horribly wrong seemed to seep into his mind and all sorts of strange ideas began to spill through his head. A rational, pragmatic academic, he was not usually prone to bouts of imagination, preferring to understand the world about him in terms of scientific laws and empirical observation. But the dark thoughts began to surface within his disciplined brain. Images of obscene burrowing things and bloated, ugly, misshapen abnormalities coalesced within his mind. Wildly cavorting eldritch shadows and gathered, torch-carrying masses danced amid these distorted monstrosities.

Savagely, he shook his head, trying to break the mental imagery created by recent events and an over-wrought imagination. He was finding it hard to come to terms with what had happened. Fragments of what seemed like a long-forgotten nightmare crawled like something hideous and unsightly into his brain, chilling him to the marrow. Fear chilled him and almost stopped the sick thudding of his heart. He was trembling now, violently, so that he could hardly stand upright. Savagely, he pulled himself together. There had to be a rational explanation. *Grown men did not just vanish into thin air*, he tried to tell himself.

He glanced down at his wristwatch, noting that it was now almost three o'clock. Matthews was taking his time. He waited in the damp chill another ten minutes then, with a curse and a shake of his head, he picked up a shovel and set off in the direction of the van.

Fear and apprehension filled that short trudge through the mud and the fog, and the feeling that he was now venturing into an unearthly place filled his troubled mind. Visibility had now reduced to almost nothing, yet some unwanted thought within his mind cried out to him that there were unseen things out there, malign and grisly things that wanted nothing more than to devour him.

Less than five minutes later, he stood, perplexed and alone, by the parked van. There were no signs of either of his associates; no bloody handprint on the door, no note tucked under the wiper blades, no nothing. He felt a part of his mind begin to shatter. With legs that had now turned to jelly, he stumbled over to the van and opened the passenger door.

There was nothing more that he could do but clamber inside.

The rain was now thundering off the van and distant

thunder rumbled, all adding to Salisbury's sense of growing unease. He reached into the back and fetched the small portable radio. Switching it on, his heart sank when all he got was static and interference. From every channel there was nothing. A further ten minutes went by and the sounds of the thunder grew louder. Distant lightning flashed in the dimness. The rest of the world could have disappeared, he thought, fiddling with the controls of the radio and getting nothing but white noise. He felt as though a long-forgotten nightmare was trying to crawl into his brain.

Knowing that it was probably better to stay inside the vehicle than venture out, Salisbury decided to try and go through some of his paperwork in an effort to drag his mind out of the current predicament. It proved hard to concentrate, and after another ten minutes or so his agitation reached breaking point. Cursing the fact that he did not carry a spare set of keys, he smashed his right fist down on the dashboard, sending the coffee flask flying.

This was not happening, he tried to tell himself. None of this was possible. The small hairs at the back of his neck prickled uncomfortably. Vainly, he tried to relax his mind, taking several deep breaths. But in spite of everything he could do, all the thoughts and the half-formed ideas came crowding back, jostling with each other, running riot through his aching skull. Everything was a swirling, raging chaos. *Where could they have gone?*

Outside, the sky was now beginning to darken to an

unhealthy indigo. In the distance, a flash of lightning flared in a whiplash of vibrant white. Then came the rumbling of thunder.

Salisbury reached under his seat for the powerful torch. Switching it on, he was relieved to find that it still worked. Nervously, he shone the beam of light into the back of the van. Dancing shadows appeared and disappeared as he focused the beam of light onto the upper torso of the bog body, which now lay enveloped in transparent plastic sheeting. A cold sensation tickled his flesh at the sight of the remains and sweat popped to his forehead. A tight knot of fear gripped his stomach, for the two-thousand-year-old remains reminded him of a hideous horror he had once seen in a freak show at a travelling fair when he was a boy. The deformed dwarf had delighted others, but had sickened him, and had given him nightmares for weeks after.

The fear and the growing apprehension was becoming unbearable. Here he was, alone in the semi-dark, his only company a stinking, unsightly, upper half of a recently unearthed bog body.

He was feeling physically sick now; his stomach churning, his nerves on edge. Taking his eyes away from the ghastly thing in the back of the van, he gazed out into the murky, wild night, thoughts of dark possibilities invading his mind. Desperately, he tried to fight off the feelings, repeatedly failing to convince himself that this was just a big hoax. In a few minutes, his friends would turn up, laughing at his expense. But, as the minutes agonisingly crept past, and the brooding darkness gathered outside, the more the gut-wrenching fear grew.

The fear threatened to tear him asunder. This was not happening, he repeatedly told himself. People don't just disappear! His mind screamed at him and madness threatened to overtake him, to possess him, to drag him away into the dark places from which there was no return.

Suddenly there was a heavy thud from behind.

Scared witless, Salisbury's eyes darted everywhere at once. Flashing the torch wildly, he noticed that a mattock had slipped from its support and now lay on the floor. Apart from that, nothing looked out of place.

With a fierce effort, he managed to keep a grip on himself. Gingerly, he reached over his seat for the handle of the nearby spade, half-expecting the now reeking corpse to leap at him or start thrashing insanely under its sheet. The horror was now becoming intolerable.

Madly, he kicked open the passenger door and sprang outside. He began waving the torch around, trying to signal to anyone that was out there. "Shaw! Matthews!" he hollered into the stormy darkness. The deep rumbling of thunder and the persistent rain, his only answer.

"*Help!* Anybody!" His voice was pleading. It was now almost fully dark. Resignedly, he got back into the van and closed the door. A tangle of incredible possibilities crashed like dark waves against his corroding rationality. In all his life, he had never been faced with anything so bizarre and unfathomable before. This went way beyond anything that he had ever experienced.

The evening crept on as he tried and failed to rest. No matter what position he got in, sleep would just not come, as though his in-built survival instincts were purposefully keeping him awake. One moment he found himself unnaturally warm, despite the fact that it must have been only a degree or two above zero. The next, he would be shivering uncontrollably as though icy-cold water was trickling down his spine.

Now free from its waterlogged grave, the damp carcass in the back of the van began to deteriorate with a stench like rotting compost.

Salisbury cursed, both at the smell and the fact that unless he acted, the find would be badly damaged by morning. Reluctantly, he clambered into the back, the torch gripped tightly. With a trembling hand, he peeled back the transparent cover and examined the leaking bog body and whilst some of his colleagues may have looked upon the remains with a feeling of sympathy, expressing some level of empathy towards it and the person it had once been, to him it was just plain ugly. To his eyes, there was nothing to which he could express any level of humanity. On the contrary, *this was death*; a preserved testimony of man's religious-induced inhumanity. For what he was looking at had undoubtedly been a sacrificial victim. Around its dishevelled, stab-wounded neck was a short length of knotted sinew. One eye-socket had been splintered and parts of the cranium jutted from the back of its head.

Its only arm resembled a large, puffy, dark sausage. The remainder was mostly skeletal or missing entirely.

The stench emanating from it bordered on the horrendous.

Swallowing a lump in his throat, Salisbury reached for the small spray-gun lying nearby and started to squirt the distilled water over the remains, moistening the skin.

It was while he was doing so that the bog body's only eye opened!

Ten, silent, horror-filled seconds passed.

Salisbury's teeth were chattering slightly as he continued to stare. Then, slowly, he regained some of his composure. With a deep breath, he reached out, tentatively running his fingers out towards the watery face. A lump gathered in his throat, but he swallowed and pushed it down with a convulsive motion of his neck muscles. Closing his eyes, his fingertips made contact with the spongy skin, feeling the ooze-like sliminess. Mustering what courage there remained within him, he gradually opened his eyes.

It's just the relaxing of the stretched skin, he tried to tell himself. Horrible as his situation was, he actually smiled. A grim smile. Slowly, the fear and the whimpering hysteria drained away, enabling him to think clearly and logically again. Breathing deeply, he tried to put things into perspective and get a grip of himself.

A sudden wet thud against the van's rear window caused his heart to leap. Spinning the torch round, Salisbury saw a ghastly, squidgy face pressed up against the back window, trailing a line of black earth in an obscene smear. Half a bloody earthworm squirmed within it.

The terrible image disappeared instantly, leaving only the square of blackness against which the wind and the rain battered.

A terror-filled scream rose within him, threatening to rush from his lungs. Fear overcame him once more; a paralysing, dark fear that threatened to destroy his mind. Desperately, he squeezed his eyes shut once more, shaking the horrible sight he had seen at the window from his consciousness. Madness was screaming far down in his mind, and it seemed that a hideous cacophony of lunatic sounds now beat at his ears. He couldn't move. His legs and arms refused to obey the instructions from his brain. A shuddering breath emptied his lungs, rasping in his mouth.

"Oh, God!" he cried. *"What's happening to me!?"* As though of its own volition, his right hand went to his head and began to tug at his hair as insanity, brought on by his dreadful experiences, began to take a deeper hold of his psyche.

For a few minutes, he just sat there, unable to do anything. Slowly, some sense of sanity began to creep back into his distraught mind. He tried to tell himself that there had been nothing at the window; that it had only been a phantasm, a hideous figment of his imagination brought on by the terrifying conditions and the worry over his missing colleagues. Maybe it had even been nothing more than his own reflection, gruesomely warped in the semi-darkness; but fear had made such an illusion more disturbingly realistic.

Alone in the torchlight, he clambered back into the passenger seat. Through the windscreen, even in the impenetrable fog and darkness he could tell that the conditions outside were getting wilder. The wind howled like a banshee.

How long he spent staring out into the desolation, he could not tell. He would spend moments holding his breath, feeling the icy fingers of fear creeping up and down his spine, believing at times that he had seen shadows moving within the deeper darkness. There's nothing there, he tried to tell himself. But deep down, he knew he was wrong. He moved his head very slowly, cautiously, from side-to-side, dreading that at any moment something unbearably horrible would suddenly appear at one of the van windows and that the mere sight of it would either kill him outright or drive him incurably insane.

He tried to tell himself that he was gripped in the coils of a dreadful, horrible dream. Something from which he would awaken, gasping for breath and lathered in cold sweat. That all he had to do was to endure it, to go with it, to see it through to its bitter end. In doing so, he was trying to trick himself into believing that, as terrible as this experience was, it could not hurt him.

That thought provided some comfort; some small piece of reassurance.

What he needed to do was to distract himself, to try

and mentally distance himself from the horrors of his predicament. Looking around him, he saw his archaeological report and he was just about to start going over it, when, faintly, he heard the sounds of dogs baying. His heart leapt.

Dogs? He rolled down the window in order to better hear. It was definitely dogs. And dogs meant farmers, he thought. And farmers meant farms, where there would be warmth and light and perhaps a telephone with which he could contact the police and the rescue teams.

Grabbing the torch, he zipped up his waterproof and opened the van door in order to step outside into the wind and the rain. The barking and the howling grew louder, yet was still somewhat far off. He stood his ground, unsure whether to call out for apprehension had now started to grow within him. These were no farm dogs he could hear approaching; this was an entire pack of ravenous, night-black, red-eyed hounds, he told himself. They had his scent and they would track him down and tear him to pieces. He had to get away. He had to.

The van would offer no safety. He had to run.

Frantic, he turned on his heels and set off, the very soil and mud now seemingly twisted and corrupted with evil, as though they possessed a malign, mischievous force which seemed to trip and cling with every boot which fell on it. Muddy water, laced with what looked like blood, bubbled, squelched, and flowed in rivulets from the befouled ground. The odd, looming form of a stunted tree would sometimes emerge before him as though possessed of its own malign spirit.

His mind was playing tricks on him, he tried to tell himself, as he dashed headlong into the darkness, the wild barking now directly behind him. Through the rain and the mud he plunged, the bog-land, with its few misshapen, lightning-scarred trees, a thoroughly hellish place. An unwholesome feeling gnawed at his nerves and pulled at his senses. It was as though he was nearing something that had lain asleep for countless ages and that he was now in danger of waking it.

A sudden finger of lightning smote a tree close by, engulfing it in flames. The air was filled with the smell of ozone.

The fog was thickening, swathing him in its ghostly shroud, smothering him in its chill embrace. Foul marsh gases belched and bubbled.

The dogs were getting nearer.

Resignedly, he turned to face them, knowing that there was no means of escape. But there was nothing there! He uttered a hysterical laugh. His heart was thudding madly against his ribs and he felt that at any moment the ghostly dogs would materialise before him. That the mist would condense, shift into solid forms with glaring, baleful red eyes, and that they would then launch themselves at him, bring him down and tear him to pieces.

He had the unsettling feeling that eyes were watching him, following his every movement, but when he swung round sharply to look, there was nothing there.

Although at times he had the unshakeable impression that someone—or something—had stood there but a fraction of a second before, and had then simply melted away into the night as though having anticipated his motion.

A hand grabbed his leg!

With a cry, Salisbury looked down.

A grotesque, slime-dripping arm had emerged from the ankle-deep quagmire, its foul hand gripped around him. Hideous, ghoul-like arms began to push their way up from the corpse-saturated bog around him. Like obscene mushrooms, terrible-looking heads, some severed completely, began to push themselves up from the ground below.

Salisbury screamed and screamed. He was still screaming as more loathsome arms grabbed him, and started pulling him down, hauling him into the blackish, watery depths. Then, through the darkness, he could see a wraith-like form drifting across the marsh towards him, its movements bizarre and frightening. Around it was a ghostly bilious glow, an eldritch effulgence which did nothing but highlight the impending horror. In one hand, it gripped a long knife.

As it neared, Salisbury could see that it was a hideous, crone-like thing, its face filled with evil. Its eyes were dark and soulless, and yet something within them burned with a hatred of all living things. Its skin was a nauseating green, broken in places with patches of mottled olive. A thing of pure nightmare.

"Three for the three taken. Three for the three taken.

Three for the three taken—" it cackled as it brought the knife down.

* * * * * * *

Sudden horror shivered along Salisbury's spine, throwing him violently from the nightmare and making him jerk bolt upright in his bed, as though he had been pulled by invisible ropes. He clenched and unclenched his fists as his breath gushed out in a shuddering gasp that emptied his lungs and made his chest ache. With wild and staring eyes, he stared about him in the cool moonlight that shone in through the bedroom window over to his right. Everything was still, and yet his whole body fizzed and tingled with that strange palpitation which comes after a close escape from danger.

The dying vestiges of the nightmare grated on his nerves and jarred through every muscle and vein of his body. He opened his mouth to scream, but nothing came out. His lips were hard and stiff, his body cold. He choked. Fiercely, he shut his eyes tightly, screwing them up, feeling them water, so that when he finally managed to open them again, it was a little difficult to see clearly.

Shadowy objects seemed to be sliding away from him as though through a rippling of dark water. He sat upright, shaking. Straining his ears, he listened, trying to detect anything out of the ordinary. The only sound was the faint rustle of leaves outside in the wind and the monotonous ticking of his wristwatch on the bedside cabinet.

The things he had witnessed in his nightmare had, if seen in reality, been enough to make a man spend the rest of his days screaming—or drive him insane. And yet, he felt he had to try and somehow resurrect the foul images in his mind; that in some way they were a warning—a premonition of the horror that was to come. Try as he might, it slipped away from him.

After an hour, in which he could not get back to sleep, he got up, dressed, and went down into his study. On the desk in front of him lay dozens of books on Iron Age archaeology, including the one that he was writing. Later that day he would be going out to investigate a possible archaeological site on the remote North Yorkshire Moors with two of his colleagues.

Now, if only he could remember that nightmare....

ARMY OF THE DAMNED

Welcome to Savetskya-Ozdok—Hell on Earth!

The dark grey shape of the military helicopter sped across the cold, dark-grey sky, the deafening chop, chop, chop of the main rotor blades cutting through the otherwise unbroken silence of the glacial desolation far below. A small red light was continually flashing, and Dmitri Savlov watched it with some concern, not knowing what it signified. For all he knew it was a warning sign meant to indicate that there was a malfunction somewhere, and that the helicopter was going to crash. However, it had now been going on for about ten minutes, and none of the other passengers seemed to be overly concerned about it, and most of them were soldiers, undoubtedly accustomed to flying in such vehicles.

He hated flying. Always had. And now here he was, in a helicopter some three thousand feet up, heading towards a top secret military base hidden in the foothills of the Ural Mountains. Since leaving Moscow a strong sense of apprehension had taken hold of him, a feeling that this mission was going to be his last, and that what he was going to witness out here would transcend all levels of normality.

As a practitioner and a top researcher in psychical and paranormal activity, he was not one to scare easily, having seen many strange and inexplicable things over the course of his career. However, the scant details he had heard at the briefing had made him extremely uneasy. If even only a half of what he had been told was true, then what he was about to participate in was something that surely existed only at the very boundaries of supernatural achievability. This would be no mere exercise in telekinesis, thought-projection, or clairvoyance, he told himself. This would be cutting edge, an unholy marriage between science and the occult.

There came some form of announcement from the helicopter pilot, but his words were drowned out by the whirling noise, so that Savlov had no idea what had been said. Watching those around him, he got the general idea and tightened his seatbelt. It seemed as though the helicopter was preparing to descend in order to land.

With a wrenching of neck muscles, Savlov craned behind him to look out of the small, porthole-like window. He could see nothing but greyness. His stomach lurched as a strong gust of wind buffeted the helicopter and he felt close to vomiting. He clenched the black briefcase that he had brought with him tighter between his knees.

Two of the soldiers seated opposite grinned and laughed uncaringly at his obvious discomfort.

Savlov closed his eyes and muttered a prayer to a god he no longer believed in as a further violent blast of wind struck the helicopter. Something heavy fell and clattered. Everything seemed to be rattling, the juddering convulsions growing in intensity as though the helicopter was about to rattle itself to pieces. At any moment, he thought the whole thing was going to disintegrate, to break up into a thousand pieces of jagged metal, and that the floor would open up and he would fall through the freezing late morning air to his doom.

The final descent was proving unbearable for him, a long, drawn-out hell of what seemed to be a never-ending downward spiral. Sweat streamed from his face and the nails of his fingers dug deep into the palms of his hands. An awful metallic stench mixed with diesel fumes that he had not noticed previously almost make him gag. A knot of fear crystallised into a hard, sinking sensation within him, and he felt his stomach rise to his gullet as the helicopter dropped further. A strong sense of impending disaster shook him to the very core of his being.

And then there came the bone-jarring thump as the helicopter landed.

Grasping his head in both hands, Savlov let out a long gasp of relief. His hands were trembling and his heart was thumping sickly against his ribs. Still, he had got here.

The real terror was yet to come.

* * * * * * *

"Greetings, comrade Savlov," said the small, bespectacled, dark-suited man. "Let me be the first to welcome you to Savetskya-Ozdok. My name is Nikolai Vhorsky, and along with General Lukovich I run this godforsaken base." There was no sincerity in his voice whatsoever. His accent was cold and unpleasant, his words seemingly dripping like slime. There was an uncanny and unwholesome paleness to his skin, and a blackness to his eyes as though he was someone who rarely saw daylight—someone who spent most of their life below ground.

Savlov shook the other's offered hand and quickly released it, for the man's skin was cold and damp and it felt as though he had just shaken hands with a corpse. He gave a curt nod. "Comrade." He shivered against the chill of the cold mountain air. Behind him, about a dozen soldiers were off-loading numerous boxes of equipment from the helicopter, and a light snow was beginning to fall. Everything seemed to be shades of white and grey, from the low-rise buildings in front of him to the towering, jagged peaks of the mountains beyond.

Vhorsky grinned. "I daresay you will find this a hell of a lot colder than your apartment in Moscow. So shall we get inside, and I'll show you to where you'll be staying." He turned and began striding purposefully across the landing pad towards a nondescript structure, ringed by a fence topped with cruel-looking razor wire, from which the hammer and sickle flag fluttered proudly, Savlov following quickly on his heels. A tall lookout tower stood nearby. And in the distance, a mile or so away, something resembling a giant radar dish was being constructed.

"I take it, then, that you now have *it*?" inquired Savlov, having to raise his voice in the gathering wind. A sudden cold chill went through him, one that was not attributed solely to the freezing temperature. His knuckles whitened around the handle of his black briefcase.

"Yes, we managed to find it several days ago. Your information regarding its whereabouts was most useful."

They were now approaching a checkpoint at which soldiers armed with Kalashnikovs and with ferocious-looking guard dogs stood sentry. The soldiers saluted as the two men passed through.

There was no denying the fact that this area was heavily militarised and Savlov held the opinion, from initial appearance anyway, that this was one of the most secure bases he had ever been to. Throughout the course of his career he had worked at numerous military and top-secret establishments, including several atomic research stations and chemical warfare plants, but there was something about Savetskya-Ozdok, and more significantly the work that was being carried out here, that clearly necessitated a heavy military and security presence.

Entering through the doors of a rather drab and uniform building, Savlov found himself in a large reception area, and it seemed that no matter where he looked there were vainglorious posters of the General Secretary. There was even a large bronze statue of him in the centre of the room. The rousing sound of *Meadowlands* was being pumped through the airwaves from the public-speaking system.

The floor was tiled with squares of black and white, and apart from the predominant Soviet artwork, there was very little else to engender any notion of aesthetic grandness or comfort. Two soldiers and a man dressed in casual clothing watched them disinterestedly from a table nearby.

For some strange reason, it seemed to Savlov as though there was an air of eerie expectancy about the room, with the dull yellow glow from the overhead lights throwing disturbing shadows everywhere. He closed his eyes, concentrating; his trained psychic mind reaching out, making itself receptive, trying to touch everything with gripping, clutching fingers. There *were* psychic disturbances here, no doubt about it. Things had happened here, perhaps not in this very room, or even in this very building; but nevertheless things had happened here, weird and supernatural things, things that defied science.

"Comrade Savlov! Are you all right?"

Savlov opened his eyes. "Yes."

"Very good. If you'd follow me, I'll show you to where you'll be staying, you can get yourself freshened up before I introduce you to General Lukovich, who I'm sure will be most pleased to meet you. It's just through this door up ahead, and then along the corridor for a bit. Your room has an excellent view overlooking the Ural Mountains. Make the most of it, for when we start work in earnest, we will be underground."

Once again Savlov felt an odd stirring, a slight tremor in the psychic field. He would be very interested to find out just what kind of experiments had been conducted here, and, of course, to have more information about the forthcoming experiment, which, if what he had been told at the initial briefing was anything to go by, proved to be unlike anything ever tried before. He was certain of this: certain that this was going to be something that even his rivals in the United States had never even contemplated. Besides, he was convinced that without *it*, all was futile.

* * * * * * *

Savlov's room was small and basic, utilitarian and rather austere, and he had expected something cosier. Nevertheless, the bed was comfortable and the washing amenities worked. Additionally, it did have, as Vhorsky had mentioned, a truly spectacular view of the neighbouring mountains.

His body felt stiff and tired despite the fact that he had rested for a couple of hours, and there were little tremors working their way along his limbs. His eyes kept flicking from one side of the room to the other, resting most of the time in the direction of the door where he expected to hear a knock sooner or later. Somewhere outside, he could hear the monotonous beeping from some alarm system or other, and on one or two occasions there had been a brief announcement over the radio system.

He got up and poured himself a coffee from the flask that, alongside a plate of salmon sandwiches, had been provided. He took a sip from the cup, feeling the glow of warmth in his throat and stomach before taking one of the sandwiches and biting into it. He had always been partial to salmon, and he was just about to take a second mouthful when—

There was a sudden, sharp stabbing pain in his brain. It was as though someone had driven a red-hot poker through his head. For an instant, the room blurred before him as he saw it through a veil of tears. Then, when he blinked them away, everything steadied for a moment. His jaw muscles were tight as he sat there, hesitant, not knowing how to react. His heart was hammering against his ribs, and a tiny germ of fear was beginning to scream thinly at the back of his mind. Panic threatened to pull his mind apart, to rip it into shreds, sending little electric tremors racing along every nerve and fibre of his body. Waiting here was no good; he needed to be active, to shake off whatever it was.

Hastily, he got himself ready, snatched up his briefcase, and left his small room. His nerves were afire, and with some effort, he steadied himself in order to force away the sensation of fear and apprehension that tugged at him, that warned him to stay well clear. He was making his way down the corridor towards the reception centre when another door creaked eerily in the semi-darkness behind him. He turned his head sharply at the unexpected sound. Narrowing his eyes, he saw Vhorsky coming towards him.

"Comrade Savlov, General Lukovich is waiting. If you can ensure that you have all of your necessities, I think it is time for us to go underground in order that we can start our preparations. If you would follow me."

The subterranean complex into which Vhorsky led Savlov was a labyrinth of dark corridors and sealed doors. Some passages were lit by overhead fluorescent lights, but most were shadowy and seemed to stretch on for an eternity, disappearing into a stygian blackness. They went through a series of security-points, passing laboratory-like rooms filled with clicking computers and white-coated scientists who worked with a certain mechanical purpose, almost as though they were automatons, state-employed robots beavering away in order to gain whatever scientific or supernatural advantage they could discover in order to obtain supremacy in an uncertain world.

"Quite some place you've got here," said Savlov, taking in his surroundings. They were not that dissimilar to a dozen other top-secret bases he had worked in, although he had the feeling that they were going to be venturing deeper, into far more secret zones.

Vhorsky spun round. "Yes, we're making some fairly important discoveries down here. I wish I had the time to give you a proper tour, for undoubtedly some of it would interest you greatly. But I'm afraid the general is waiting. However, I can tell you that our researchers have already managed to isolate several of the brainwaves linked to thought manipulation. We're also making great strides in the fields of telepathy and remote listening and detecting—I daresay I need not go on, for, after all, it was through your psychical ability that we managed to pinpoint the exact epicentre of the Tunguskan explosion in order to extract the tiny sample of extraterrestrial matter which will be of fundamental importance in the experiment."

"And was it residual anti-matter, as some have suggested?" There was obvious curiosity in Savlov's voice. "Or was the fragment merely meteoric?"

"Our initial investigations have shown that it was not anti-matter. Nor was it simply meteoric in origin. Using some of our Tesla devices and our breakthroughs in radio-chromatography, we have managed to establish that it is partly formed from what we are terming 'chaos-matter,' and partly from an as yet unidentifiable mineral crystal which is composed of no known terrestrial elements."

"Interesting."

"Yes, extremely." Keying in a long code on the security pad, Vhorsky opened another door. "We're now venturing into what I like to think of as the innermost sanctum. Once inside, we will go into my office where we will meet the general." He turned to look at Savlov, a slightly deranged look now on his face. "This is where we will make history, Comrade Savlov. This is where the first steps to restore the greatness of the motherland will start."

Savlov was lost for words. How could he respond to that? With a slight nod of his head, he indicated for the other to lead on.

Vhorsky's office was wide and spacious, with a full-length, floor to ceiling one-way mirror dominating one wall. It enabled those inside to see, in privacy, into the adjacent chamber, which at first glance made Savlov think of an interrogation room or a cell within a lunatic asylum. A long table lay within, and Vhorsky walked over to one of the chairs placed around it and motioned Savlov towards it. "Please be seated," he said, "while I go and inform the general that you're here."

Savlov walked in and took his place even as Vhorsky exited through a side door. There was a faint light in the room coming from some source close to the ceiling, but it was bright enough for him to make out the overall bareness of the room.

Once more, he felt that tug at his mind, as though some entity from nearby was trying to enter and control his thoughts, to make contact in a negative way. He had an eerie sensation of eyes watching quietly, yet somehow amusedly, from somewhere nearby. He tried desperately to keep from looking around.

There was no doubt in his mind that something was trying to make some kind of connection with him. It was almost as though whatever it was had realised the role he was about to play in the forthcoming experiment, and was trying to persuade him, to manipulate him, in some manner regarding the experiment's final outcome.

It was as he was worrying over these matters that the door through which Vhorsky had left opened, and he returned, pushing a wheelchair, in which slumped a deathly-grey and sick-looking individual dressed in a military uniform pinned with many medals and wearing a peaked cap with the Soviet red star. The seated individual looked terrible; the eyes were white where the pupils had rolled back in the head. He looked more dead than alive.

Savlov was confused. "Where's the general?" he asked. "Surely—"

Vhorsky gave a cold smile. "May I introduce General Lukovich. There's no need to salute." His grin widened, revealing his madness to full effect. "He's been looking forward to meeting you." From the back of the wheelchair, he removed two lengths of thin cable that had small probes at the ends. "I'll just plug him in." With that, he removed the cap.

The top of the general's scalp had been removed, peeled back, revealing the exposed brain.

Savlov felt his knees buckle and a gasp of horror rose to his lips as he witnessed Vhorsky push the twin probes into small sockets which protruded from the gelatinous brain. Something within him seemed to implode, to darken his thoughts and send him over the edge. Inwardly, his commonsense screamed at him, telling him that this was not happening. A running riot stampeded unchecked through his brain and every-thing was a whirling, raging chaos. For a time, he stood stock still, trying to comprehend what it was he was looking at, to try and impose some level of rationality on it. But it was no good. Despite all of the strangeness that he had seen and had believed in, this was something that could not be comprehended so easily. It was an abomination.

"Well, aren't you at least going to say hello?" In a parody of affection, Vhorsky patted the corpse on the shoulder. He threw Savlov an uncertain glance. "Now, don't go telling me that you're shocked. I'd have thought that a man of your background and especially one of your profession would have been able to accept and indeed wonder at the general's current situation. He can hear, see, taste, smell, and touch. He retains some mental faculty and, aside from myself, is one of the operational heads of the current project. I expect you to offer him your full cooperation. Otherwise, he might bite you." Vhorsky gave a shrill laugh. It was blatantly clear that he was thoroughly insane.

"What happened?" Savlov found that he could not take his eyes off the thing in the wheelchair, no matter how much he wished he could. "General Lukovich was a bear of a man, a distinguished leader—how can it be that he's been reduced to—*this?*"

"The answer's very simple, I killed him." Vhorsky stared hard at Savlov. "It was not murder, I can assure you, but rather self-preservation and a devotion to the motherland. You see, the general wanted to have this base of operations closed down. I think he saw little use in what we were achieving here. He was a military man and had little faith in what we were doing.

When I informed him of my plan, he at first ridiculed it entirely, resigning it to mere mumbo-jumbo. He was a fool, unable to fully grasp the potential that was at our fingertips."

"So you—you killed him?"

"Well, not in the strictest sense. Yes—he is dead. But I've been able to rewire much of his sensory and nervous system. With the help of the circuitry I've installed throughout his body, just with the mere flick of a switch I can, to some extent, reanimate him. I also believe that he still maintains some residual thought process. I'm sure I've heard him muttering, at night, even when he's not switched on."

Savlov shuddered at the very thought. Fighting back the repulsiveness that wanted to dominate him, he crouched down and stared long and hard at the dead man. But was he dead, or was he merely existing in some half-life, some shadowy in-between, some vague phantom realm between life and death, Heaven and Hell? He drew in a sharp breath as he saw the other man's features, broad and jowled, in the glare from the overhead lights.

Savlov cautiously reached out with his mind to the general. Perhaps this wretched thing was the entity that had touched his mind earlier.

There was nothing. Not even the background hum he got from any normal human.

He could not understand how life was being maintained; however, the sensory inputs and brain-wave analysis machine resting to one side however showed steady activity.

"General Lukovich, can you hear me?"

The eyes flickered and the lips trembled, forming soundless words.

"He's trying to speak," said Savlov. "Is there any way in which—"

"Ah, my apologies. I'll just up the power a little." Vhorsky threw a couple of switches on the electronic box attached to the back of the wheelchair, and placed a small microphone to the general's lips.

Suddenly the general jerked into some semblance of life. He was like a puppet, the strings replaced with computerised wiring. His pupils rolled down, and he looked around with curiosity as though unsure of his surroundings. His right arm began to tremble as a jolt of electricity shot through it. "I welcome you to Savetskya-Ozdok, Comrade Savlov. I hope your journey here was pleasant. Vhorsky has informed me that you're a leading authority on occult and paranormal study and that you're the man for the job. Excellent." The voice sounded highly mechanical, computerised, inhuman. It sounded like the echo of someone talking into a tin can. "I trust that you keep in your briefcase the formulae needed to complete the ritual. There's a lot of responsibility riding on us here, as you undoubtedly know."

Savlov found it hard not to wince. He merely nodded, unable to gather the strength of will to speak back. How could he have a conversation with this? He felt as though the fabric of his sanity was being chipped away, and that sooner or later it would crumble completely. Thoughts, burning questions, spilled into his brain in a whirling chaos. What exactly was this? Curiosity, caution, and fear battled for supremacy in his mind. Curiosity forced him to go on with this, to go forward and see where it would take him. Caution instructed him to be wary, to admit to himself that this was something far beyond his previous experience. And fear was there too, because of the dark, evil things that seemed to be associated with all that was happening.

A terrible, nauseous impression began to encroach on Savlov, filling his brain and his very being like black smoke. He retched as the feeling grew stronger within him. There was a sudden tightening in the pit of his stomach, and the feeling that there was something approaching that he didn't like one bit, a grim foreboding of evil that seemed to emanate from every shadow-filled corner. The lights in the room flickered.

"Now, I understand that you were given some kind of briefing regarding the purpose of the experiment?" inquired Vhorsky. "No doubt you were told that we were conducting tests into engineering 'super soldiers' who are impervious to pain." He fiddled briefly with some of the controls on the wheelchair, none of which seemed to have any obvious impact on the seated being. He looked up. "The general here is as far as we got down that path. Not quite what Moscow wants, I think you'd agree. However, my ambitions have always been of a slightly greater magnitude. My interest in the occult and the paranormal has been driven by the strong desire to create an army of such capability that none can stand in our way; an army not only immune to death, or one incapable of knowing the meaning of fear, but one actually forged in Hell—*an Army of Demons!*"

"You're—you're insane!" cried Savlov.

"*Insane*? Where's the insanity in using whatever means one has in one's arsenal in order to gain supremacy? Don't be so naive, Comrade Savlov, to think that our enemies would hesitate to use such weaponry, such technology, such capability against us if they had the means to do so."

"You mention an army of demons—but I see nothing."

"Ah, but this is where your talents come in. You see, I've been doing a lot of my own research out here, and I believe I've found the means of creating such beings by fusing the two main principles that govern our existence. Reality and unreality. The normal and the paranormal. By utilising the Tunguskan relic and employing your mastery of Black Magic, I fervently believe that we can open a rift within the fabric of reality, to engineer a portal that will enable us to gain access to Hell."

Savlov managed not to laugh with hysteria at this crazed, murdering fool. He knew his only chance of survival lay in appeasing Vhorsky until he could escape. "And just how do you propose to control these demons?" He forced himself to keep his voice level.

"I find it strange that you're asking me this question.

Is that not your field of expertise?"

Savlov nodded wearily. "Yes, I suppose it is."

"Well then, perhaps it is time to put our plans into operation. From here, we'll go to the main laboratory where everything awaits you."

* * * * * *

"I hope you realise that I've only done this once before," said Savlov, shivering at the memory of that last time. It had been done on the outskirts of Leningrad, and it had caused him nightmares for months afterwards. All of the other participants who had been there at the time were now rotting in lunatic asylums. Hands trembling, he opened his black briefcase and started to remove a weird collection of materials, placing them on a counter on which several computers were arrayed. There were several age-yellowed scrolls of papyri, an old and crumbling leather bound book entitled *Daemonic Workings of Ipsissimus Zegrembi*, and a small velvet pouch that contained an assorted collection of coloured chalk and five black candles.

"And now you'll do it again." Vhorsky stood to one side and watched, his right hand resting on the handles of the wheelchair in which the general lay slumped. "We have full confidence in your abilities, haven't we, general?"

The general had been temporarily switched off in order to conserve electricity, so, thankfully, at least as far as Savlov was concerned, he did not reply.

In the dim yellow light from the overhead fluorescent tubes, Savlov began to mark out the shape of the Pentagram, following the exact plans given on one of the scrolls of papyrus. It was a lengthy, drawn-out procedure that took him almost an hour to complete. His jaw muscles were tight, and the growing sense of fear had returned to the pit of his stomach by the time he inscribed the last arcane sigil. He still had no idea how he would escape Vhorsky's wrath if the procedure did not work, or how to survive the results if it did. He lit the five small black candles and placed them at the corners. They gave off a repellent and oleaginous stink. He finished by circumscribing a circle around it.

"Very good." Vhorsky stood, looking down, taking in every detail.

"If you give me the Tunguskan fragment, I'll place it in the centre."

"No, I'll do it." Vhorsky walked over to a locked cabinet that had been set into the wall of the laboratory. He inserted his pass-key and pressed in a code on a number pad. He then went and put on a pair of heavy-looking safety gauntlets and opened the cabinet, returning with a cylindrical, orange gas-filled glass tube inside which pulsed a vibrant, violet light.

Savlov stared in amazement. So this was the crystal of 'chaos-matter' which had caused the massive explosion in Tunguska some fifty years before, in June 1908, devastating an area of some eight hundred and thirty square miles with a detonation force of fifteen megatons of TNT—an explosion over a thousand times greater than the atomic blast over Hiroshima. And now, at this very moment in time, it was in the hands of someone who was completely insane. A worrying thought indeed.

"As you can see, there's still a lot of activity remaining. Our scientists have managed to contain it in a partial vacuum, although they fear that there's constant isotopic disintegration, resulting in relatively strong alpha and beta-wave radiation emission. I would hate to think what would happen if I were to drop it." Suddenly, Vhorsky pretended to trip.

Savlov felt his heart leap.

"Hah! I'm only kidding." Vhorsky crossed over into the Pentagram and rested the glass cylinder in the centre. He then walked clear in order to join Savlov. "Ready when you are," he said.

Savlov stepped to the edge of the Pentagram and began to intone words from the foul grimoire he had brought with him. These were dark and unholy words, words that in the course of human history few had ever dared utter, and for good reason.

Slowly, demonic forms and shapes began to swirl and cavort within the Pentagram, wispy, ethereal tendrils of hideous smoke filled with some kind of malign purpose, some terrible hunger which strained to reach out with clawed hands. Unearthly faces materialised from within the hellish cloud. They were so alive and venomous that the two men instinctively pulled back a couple of steps.

"We're safe as long as we remain outside the Pentagram." Regardless of what he had just said,

Savlov shuddered at the sight of the infernal conglomeration of horror that was manifesting itself before his eyes. "These are just the souls of soldiers who have died here." He continued reading from the book. A ghostly, unearthly noise was now shrieking at his ears, almost drowning out everything else. It was a terrible sound, which had in it all the moaning shrieks of souls in torment in the lowest pit of hell. In spite of the tight hold he had on himself, he shuddered and felt his face grow cold. He knew that the things taking shape before him were evil and intent on his destruction.

And then the glass cylinder shattered!

A powerful shockwave knocked Savlov and Vhorsky off their feet.

Getting to his feet, Savlov was relieved to note that the entities were still confined to the Pentagram. And as he watched, a glittering, dark purple point of light sparked into existence, about which the demonic shapes began to revolve in a dizzying, frenzied dance of the dammed. There was a perverse enchantment in this phantasmagoria as the spinning picked up momentum, the circling now becoming a spiral as the glowing point of brilliance began to draw them in. Like drowning sailors caught in a whirlpool, the dammed were dragged towards the centre, the glowing orb of 'chaos-matter' flaring with each one taken. Some of the dammed tried in vain to escape, their horrible faces tortured in agony. They were suffering a torment beyond death itself.

A sudden violent tremor, like that from an earthquake, shuddered through the entire room. An over-head light snapped clear off its mooring, fell and shattered on the ground nearby.

"What's happening?" Vhorsky stared all around him with wild eyes.

"I—"

Before Savlov could reply, the laboratory darkened, causing him look around in alarm. The only light was now coming from that single point that hovered within the Pentagram, throwing grotesque shadows, and bathing the two men in a hellish, lurid, violet glow.

The violet aura changed as the glowing point began to expand, assuming a redder colour. Then, with a great splintering sound, it seemed as though the very fabric of reality had been ruptured, torn asunder, and the laboratory filling with an eerie effulgence. A series of crimson flashes came from within the swirling void that now spilled, black and oily, from whatever hellish dimension they had foolishly opened. And then, from out of the chaotic maelstrom there flew a ghastly mouth filled with row upon row of gnashing, shark-like teeth. Two, then three, then half a dozen of the hideous, snapping, disembodied jaws emerged before them, all mercifully contained within the Pentagram. For the time being at least.

"The Gateway! We've opened the portal!" Vhorsky stared, fixedly. "We've done it!"

The fanged entities were now battering at the protec-tive circle, trailing lines of slime were they tried to break free, smearing the invisible barrier with their sticky secretions.

"I can't hold them!" cried Savlov. Even as he spoke, something else burst free from the dimension beyond—a great puckered, purplish tentacle. It was soon followed by more, and then a writhing, squirming mass, like a multitude of ravenous magnets, vomited forth. Amorphous and horrible beyond all mortal comprehension, this hellish demon-spawn slithered from its extra-dimensional abode, death and horror its sole purpose. Cracks began to show in the protective barrier.

Vhorsky greeted it all with jubilation. "We've done it! We've done it!" he cried ecstatically.

"No! They'll destroy us all! We must stop them!" With that thought in mind, Savlov flicked hurriedly through the pages of the grimoire and began to mouth the incantation of dispelling. His words were forced, and he stood there for what seemed an eternity, feeling the cold, stark horror washing over him. Fear hammered at his body, shaking him to the very core of his being. He stood rigid, not daring to move as the blood pounded incessantly in his temple and brought a tense, tight feeling at the back of his eyes. His heart was palpitating madly behind his ribs, bringing a sick feeling to his stomach. His legs trembled. For a long moment, he could scarcely stand upright. The fear and the terror and the blinding horror grew so big that it was beginning to dissolve his mind. It almost unseated his reason. Then, he managed to catch himself, to draw himself into some semblance of awareness. Unless he were able to somehow master this horror that was unfolding before his very eyes, it would drive him insane. He would fall to pieces, unable to even try and defend himself.

Another great crack appeared down the protective barrier. It would only be a matter of time for the demons who had now spilled from Hell to break through the last line of defence and pour out, contaminating all with their nightmarish presence. They would all die, of that Savlov was certain. He had to try and stop it. Only a certain verse contained within the Zegrembi spell-book contained the power required. It was all just a question of whether or not he had the mental capacity and the aptitude to recite it. Given the current turmoil that was raging, he doubted it.

He found the spell and began reading, intoning the mystic words that had been recorded almost five hundred years ago. The incantation was having some effect, for the vortex began to contract. There was a scream from something unutterably diabolical. The great tentacle withdrew upon itself, dragged back within the vortex.

"What are you doing?" shouted Vhorsky.

"I have to close it or else we're all doomed! The demons are too strong. Only a sacrifice will stop them now."

Vhorsky shielded his eyes from the lightning and the dark flashing. "Perhaps we can still put the general to good use. Who knows, perhaps he will prove more useful in death than he was in life? Here's your sacrifice!" In an act of sheer madness, he pushed the wheelchair containing the general across the outer barrier of the Pentagram and into the midst of the raging chaos. The wheelchair skidded and toppled over, throwing the seated cyborg into the centre. He landed with a crash. Clashing, violet lightning flashed all around as whatever evil power resided within targeted him.

"What have you done?" shouted Savlov. "He's not a living sacrifice!"

Wreathed in a chaotic column of tortured spirits, the half-dead general was raised into the air. Caught within the midst of the daemonic cyclone, he began to spin, screaming and twirling. For one terrible moment he convulsed, as from the nebulous void something beyond all mortal comprehension tried to haul him back, to claim him, to pull him into Hell. His body was blackening and dissolving, bursting and popping as the demonic energies raged through his body. The twin probes that had been inserted into his brain glowed white hot and then exploded. Blood began to pour down his face in hideous rivulets.

This surpassed anything Savlov had ever witnessed. Hypnotised by the terrible insanity of all that was transpiring before him, he found himself unable to recite the words necessary to dispel the evil and close the Gateway. He could hear the thing that was now the general speaking in an empty voice, lonely and strangely faraway. It was a voice that spoke tales of death and the more horrible things that could come after, of screaming torture, of Hell itself. It told of the revenge that might come from those who hadn't really died, but lived on in some terrible way, still able to destroy.

Savlov was only dimly aware that Vhorsky had now retreated to the doorway. He himself pulled back further as before him the hellish entity absorbed the last of the damned souls. Its eyes had now become like glowing red coals, twin points of lambent hatred. Its hands became rigid, livid, claw-like. And then it turned to look directly at him, and for a moment he felt his soul freeze.

* * * * * * *

It was walking, stalking, crying out profanities some-where in the darkness behind them. It had crossed the protective barrier with ease and now it seemed unstop-pable. Their only hope was to run, to flee the night-mare that followed them.

"We must get out of here," shouted Vhorsky. Throwing wide the door to his office, he dashed over to his desk and withdrew an automatic handgun from a drawer. "Follow me, Comrade Savlov, if you value your life."

"I value my soul more," replied Savlov. He glanced behind him to ensure that the demonic general was not close by. He then turned to Vhorsky. "Lead on."

The two men then made a dash for it out of the office and along one of the corridors leading to the lifts which led up and out, to the relative sanity of the outside. They were now passing through areas peopled with scientists who looked at them oddly, clearly unsure as to why they were in such a hurry.

Savlov noted traces of alarm in some of the looks they got. "Should we not warn the others?" he asked as they rushed through one such complex.

"No. Hopefully, they will slow down our pursuit. This is a race for survival and one that I intend to win. Now hurry, if you too want to see daylight again."

They dashed down another long stretch of corridor, the sound of distant screams echoing from behind them.

"If we can make it to the surface, then we can get into one of the helicopters," said Vhorsky.

"You can pilot those things?"

"Yes. Now come on."

The sudden sound of an alarm began to ring, announcing that some major event was now occurring within the subterranean complex. The overhead lights dimmed.

"Hopefully the auxiliary power will stay on." Vhorsky threw open a door and sped off, violently knocking aside a technician who carried a tray of test tubes. "The elevator's just up here. Run!"

Savlov ran past the white-coated man who was beginning to clamber to his feet and sped after Vhorsky. His heart was pounding savagely in his chest like a caged animal eager for release, and sweat dampened his shirt and forehead. His nerves were tingling as tiny electric currents shot through them and a massing of pressures was throbbing at his temples. He doubted whether he had ever been as frightened in all of his life. For here he was, fleeing alongside some madman from something that went beyond evil—a living hell incarnate, a half-man, half-demon entity—a *Daemondamned*, a being whose sole purpose, it seemed, was to wreak a terrible vengeance on all that lived.

Vhorsky crashed against the elevator doors just as the lights dimmed further. "Damn!" He cursed fiercely as he desperately tried the buttons on the lift panel and found that none worked. "This power shortage has put the lift out of action. It's not working. We'll have to take the stairs. Come on: there's no time to waste."

From behind them came the sound of sporadic gunfire and then something that sounded like a grenade going off, although it could have been just an explosion in one of the laboratories.

Vhorsky's face creased at the sounds of destruction and chaos. Sweat was running profusely down his face, but that mad look in his eyes was still strong.

"This is an emergency! Would all non-essential personnel make their way to the designated evacuation points," announced a robotic-sounding voice over the public address system. "This is an emergency—" It was suddenly cut short. And then a terrible, unearthly voice said: "This is General Lukovich. All personnel of Soviet base Savetskya-Ozdok are to be terminated. I repeat, all personnel of Soviet base Savetskya-Ozdok are to be terminated."

"*Hell!* We must escape." Vhorsky stared all around him, mentally trying to deduce which was the quickest and safest way to the stairs. "This way." He turned and began running.

This was now a living nightmare, and one from which Savlov felt he was never going to escape. An unholy terror, created by the fusion of technology and Black Magic, was running amok, and he knew of no way of stopping it, no spells which could bind it or force it back to the hellish dimension from which it had come. Their foolish act had brought it into existence, and now its only purpose was to kill them—to kill them all.

Down a shadowy stretch of corridor they ran, the emergency stairs now visible at the far end, some hundred yards away. Suddenly a burst of automatic fire came from behind them. Turning, they saw two soldiers retreating from an approaching fog-like mass that billowed before them. In the smoke, figures could be seen shambling, their faces green and contorted as though they had been gassed. The soldiers pulled back further, shooting round after round into the unstoppable horror. Their ammunition now spent, they turned and fled towards where Savlov and Vhorsky were.

"It's the dead. That devil's bringing them back to life. We must get out of here," cried one of the soldiers.

"It's absolute carnage down there. All hell's broken loose." The other soldier stared about him with wide, horror-filled eyes.

"We're near the stairs now. We can get out to the surface this way." Vhorsky led them, Savlov and the two soldiers bringing up the rear.

There was fear stamped on every man's face as they started up the stairs. The lights flickered on and off, and the sounds of shouts and screams rang out from down below. It sounded as though whatever was in pursuit was fast gaining ground on them, and it was desperation that drove them on, to overcome the physical tiredness that was now beginning to bite deep. They all knew that to stop now meant certain death—and perhaps a fate worse than death. And then the lights came on fully, the intensity of the lights almost blinding, as though a great electrical surge had taken place.

Savlov was certain that at any moment the lights would overheat and explode. And then, some distance away, he heard the lifts starting up again.

Two terrible thoughts struck Savlov. The first was that now that the lifts were working, perhaps the demons could get faster access to the surface, reaching it before them. In which case they were going from the frying pan into the fire. And secondly, what if the forces on the surface had sealed off the lower levels? Such a drastic action was commonplace at many of the other top-secret bases he had worked at. It was a safety mechanism, which enabled the isolation of certain parts, a means to contain whatever threats, be they nuclear or chemical—or demonic—endangered the wider complex.

How they kept going, Savlov did not know, but it was with some relief that he saw the doors which led to the surface now in front of them. His leg muscles were throbbing painfully, and it felt as though his heart was going to implode at any moment. Then, out of the corner of his eye, he saw one of the soldiers being snatched from behind. He turned and saw the unfortunate being pulled down by a white-coated zombie.

Screaming, Savlov, Vhorsky, and the remaining soldier rushed through the doors and out into another stretch of corridor. Mercifully, this one was lined with windows through which a dim greyness, the light of early morning, filtered. At the end of the corridor, tantalisingly close yet at the same time so far away, was a set of doors leading outside.

"We're nearly there!" cried Vhorsky, running for all he was worth. He flung open the outer doors.

Standing before him was General Lukovich!

The thing looked truly horrendous, diabolical, a construct formed in the bottommost pit of Hell. No longer confined to a wheelchair, the general stood tall and solid, a uniform-jacketed hulk of pure cybernetic and demonic malignity, its face twisted with an uncontrollable rage. Little sparks danced and flickered from its exposed brain and a glowing green electric field crackled all around it. "Vhorsky!" it groaned.

Paralysed with terror, Vhorsky could do nothing as the monster grabbed him, raised him into the air and tore his head from his body.

What happened next passed in a nightmarish blur for Savlov. His mind darkened as the sheer horror and the unbelievabilty of it all began to truly take hold. He was only vaguely aware of himself and the soldier smashing their way through one of the corridor windows and running out into the cold, the wind, and the snow. Through a blizzard-raging chaos of screams, gunfire, and explosions they fought their way, heading for the helicopter landing pad. They could see soldiers frantically waving them on, urging them to hurry as the great rotor blades of the sole remaining helicopter began to turn. And then they were clambering inside. The helicopter doors were flung shut and—

Something smashed into the side, causing the metal to buckle. Savlov yelled as did some of the worried-looking soldiers crammed inside. The helicopter lurched to one side, tried to gain altitude, and then thumped back to the ground. Again came that terrible smash.

"They're trying to get in!" a soldier shouted.

At the small window behind which the soldier sat, the gruesome face of the general suddenly appeared, a triumphant grin now twisting his wicked, monstrous features.

A shudder of fear went through Savlov. Even now, when escape had seemed possible, the horrors of Savetskya-Ozdok were going to claim him as they had already claimed so many. Once more the side of the helicopter was battered by some superhuman strength.

Twirling in a great circle, they began to rise once more. Yet still the general clung to the outside, trying to force his way in, to down the helicopter and bring death to them all, to then use his demonic powers to infest them with a hellish parody of life, to turn them into *daemondamned* as he himself had been.

And then by some miracle they were free. Whether the general had missed his hold or something had given way, Savlov could not tell, but they were now truly airborne, gaining height. He had no doubt that the half-robot, half-demon had survived the fall, even though it would have killed a normal human being. Similarly, he had no doubt that whatever survivors remained at the military base would not survive for much longer. He and the soldiers in the helicopter were the fortunate few.

"I've just put through a call to headquarters in Moscow," came the voice of the pilot. "They're going to launch a nuclear strike at Savetskya-Ozdok. We should be clear of the blast radius within ten minutes."

Savlov clamped his head in his trembling hands. Inwardly, he was thinking that even an atomic bomb would prove ineffectual against what he knew was back there. He had this image in his head of the base obliterated, reduced to a radioactive wasteland yet within which General Lukovich and his undead army still existed. They did not live and they could not die, and it was only a question of time before they spread out further, an unstoppable, demonic contagion hell-bent on destruction.

The helicopter sped on.

ABOUT THE AUTHOR

As penance for past deeds, Edmund Glasby grew up in Morecambe and studied Egyptian Archaeology at University College London and Archaeology and Anthropology at Oxford. Morecambe, which has more than its share of the strange and unsavoury, provided him with a better education. After turning his back on academia, he now writes in the genres of dark fantasy and supernatural thriller, having been brought up on horror; his father was John Glasby, the prolific supernatural writer.

In 2010, his first novel was *Disciple of a Dark God*, a far-ranging dark fantasy epic. As editor, he was the compiler of *The Thing in the Mist: Selected Stories of John S. Glasby,* a forthcoming memorial tribute volume to his father. *The Dyrysgol Horror* is his first collection of supernatural stories and is a Borgo Press original, and further collections are in preparation

When he is not writing, he is the captain of a local archery club, and he has won a trophy or two both at local and European level with the English longbow he made.